Barbie™

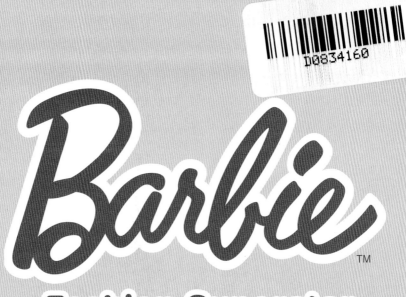

Fashion Superstar

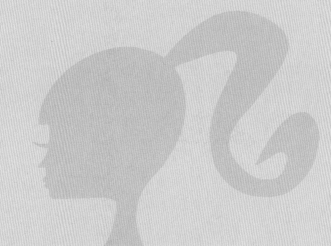

MORE GREAT GRAPHIC NOVEL SERIES AVAILABLE FROM PAPERCUTZ

Barbie
Fashion Superstar
PAPERCUTZ

BARBIE #1

Barbie
PUPPY PARTY
PAPERCUTZ

BARBIE PUPPY PARTY

ANNE of GREEN BAGELS
Susan Schade
Jon Buller
PAPERCUTZ

ANNE OF GREEN BAGELS #1

TinkerBell
PAPERCUTZ

DISNEY FAIRIES #18

JOHN STEVEN GURNEY
Fuzzy Baseball

FUZZY BASEBALL

GARFIELD
APPRENTICE SORCERER
PAPERCUTZ

THE GARFIELD SHOW #6

The Lunch Witch
PAPERCUTZ

THE LUNCH WITCH #1

MINNIE & DAISY
BEST FRIENDS FOREVER
PAPERCUTZ

MINNIE & DAISY #1

Nancy Drew
DIARIES
CAROLYN KEENE
PAPERCUTZ

NANCY DREW DIARIES #7

THE RED SHOES
AND OTHER TALES
METAPHROG
PAPERCUTZ

THE RED SHOES

Scarlett
Star on the Run
PAPERCUTZ

SCARLETT

The Sisters
PAPERCUTZ

THE SISTERS #1

SMURFS
THE WILD SMURF
PAPERCUTZ

THE SMURFS #21

Thea Stilton
THE THEA SISTERS
MYSTERY AT SEA
PAPERCUTZ

THEA STILTON #6

DREAMWORKS
Trolls
Hugs & Friends
PAPERCUTZ

TROLLS #1

THE SMURFS, MINNIE & DAISY, DISNEY FAIRIES, THE GARFIELD SHOW, BARBIE and TROLLS graphic novels are availabl
for $7.99 in paperback, and $12.99 in hardcover. THEA STILTON graphic novels are
available for $9.99 in hardcover only. FUZZY BASEBALL and NANCY DREW DIARIES graphic novels are available for
$9.99 in paperback only. THE LUNCH WITCH, SCARLETT, and ANNE OF GREEN BAGELS graphic novels are available fc
$14.99 in paperback only. THE RED SHOES graphic novel is available for $12.99 in hardcover only.
Available from booksellers everywhere. You can also order online from www.papercutz.com. Or call 1-800-886-1223,
Monday through Friday, 9–5 EST. MC, Visa, and AmEx accepted. To order by mail, please add $4.00 for postage and
handling for first book ordered, $1.00 for each additional book and make check payable to NBM Publishing.
Send to: Papercutz, 160 Broadway, Suite 700, East Wing, New York, NY 10038.

THE SMURFS, THE GARFIELD SHOW, BARBIE, TROLLS, THEA STILTON, FUZZY BASEBALL,
THE LUNCH WITCH, NANCY DREW DIARIES, THE RED SHOES, ANNE OF GREEN BAGELS, and SCARLETT
graphic novels are also available wherever e-books are sold.

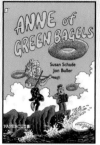

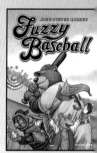

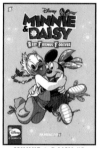

Barbie™

#1 "Fashion Superstar"

PAPERCUTZ™

NEW YORK

#1 "Fashion Superstar"

SARAH KUHN – Writer
ALITHA MARTINEZ – Artist
MATT HERMS – Colorist (cover)
LAURIE E. SMITH – Colorist
JANICE CHIANG – Letterer

DAWN GUZZO – Design/Production
JEFF WHITMAN – Production Coordinator
BETHANY BRYAN – Editor
JEFF WHITMAN – Assistant Managing Editor
JIM SALICRUP
Editor-in-Chief

Special thanks to Ryan Ferguson, Debra Mostow Zakarin, Kristine Lombardi, Sammie Suchland, Stuart Smith, Charnita Belcher, Nicole Corse, and Karen Painter

ISBN: 978-1-62991-587-6 paperback edition
ISBN: 978-1-62991-588-3 hardcover edition

Papercutz books may be purchased for business or promotional use. For information on bulk purchases please contact Macmillan Corporate and Premium Sales Department at (800) 221-7945 x5442.

Printed in Canada
September 2016 by Marquis

Distributed by Macmillan
First Printing

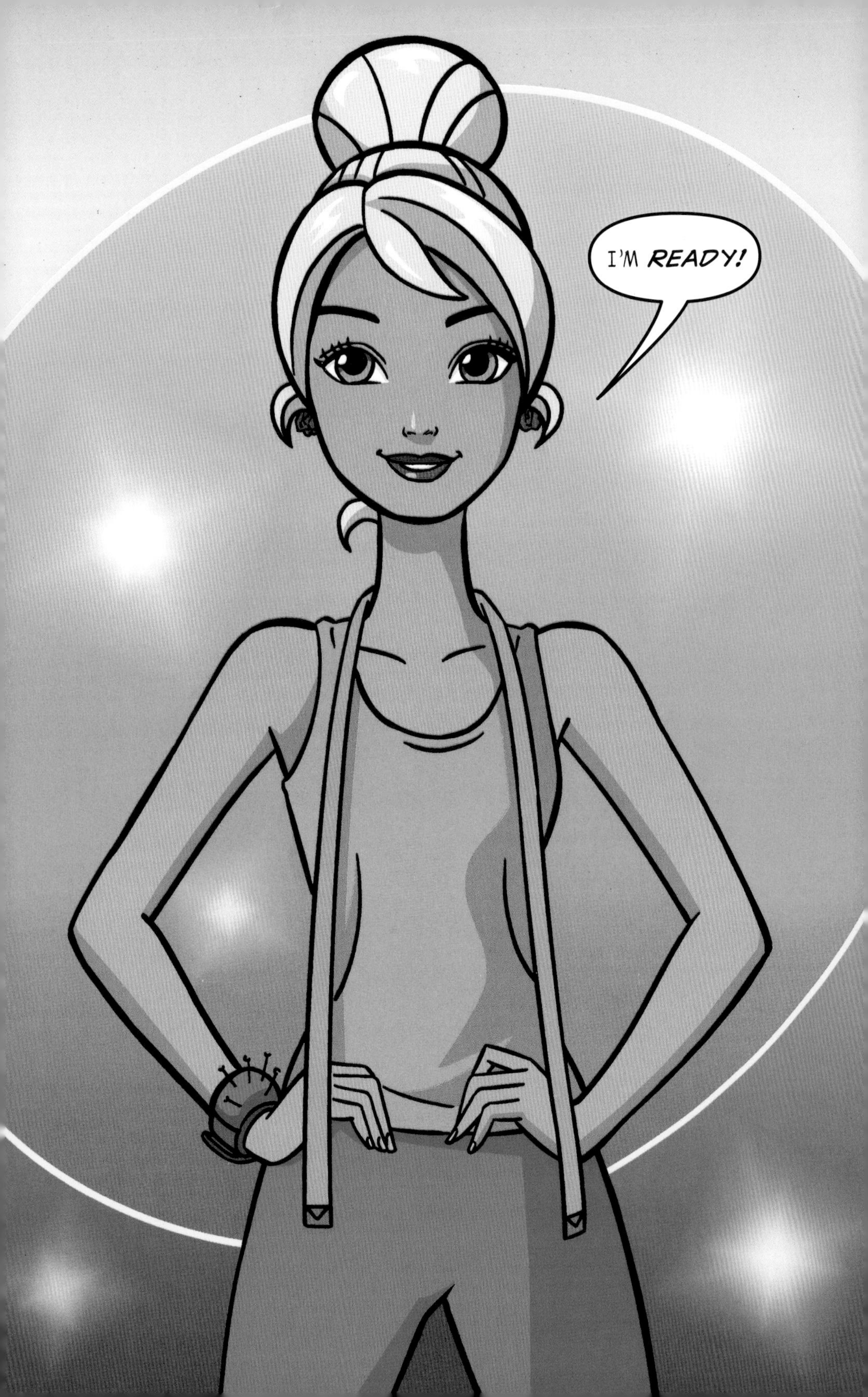
I'M *READY!*

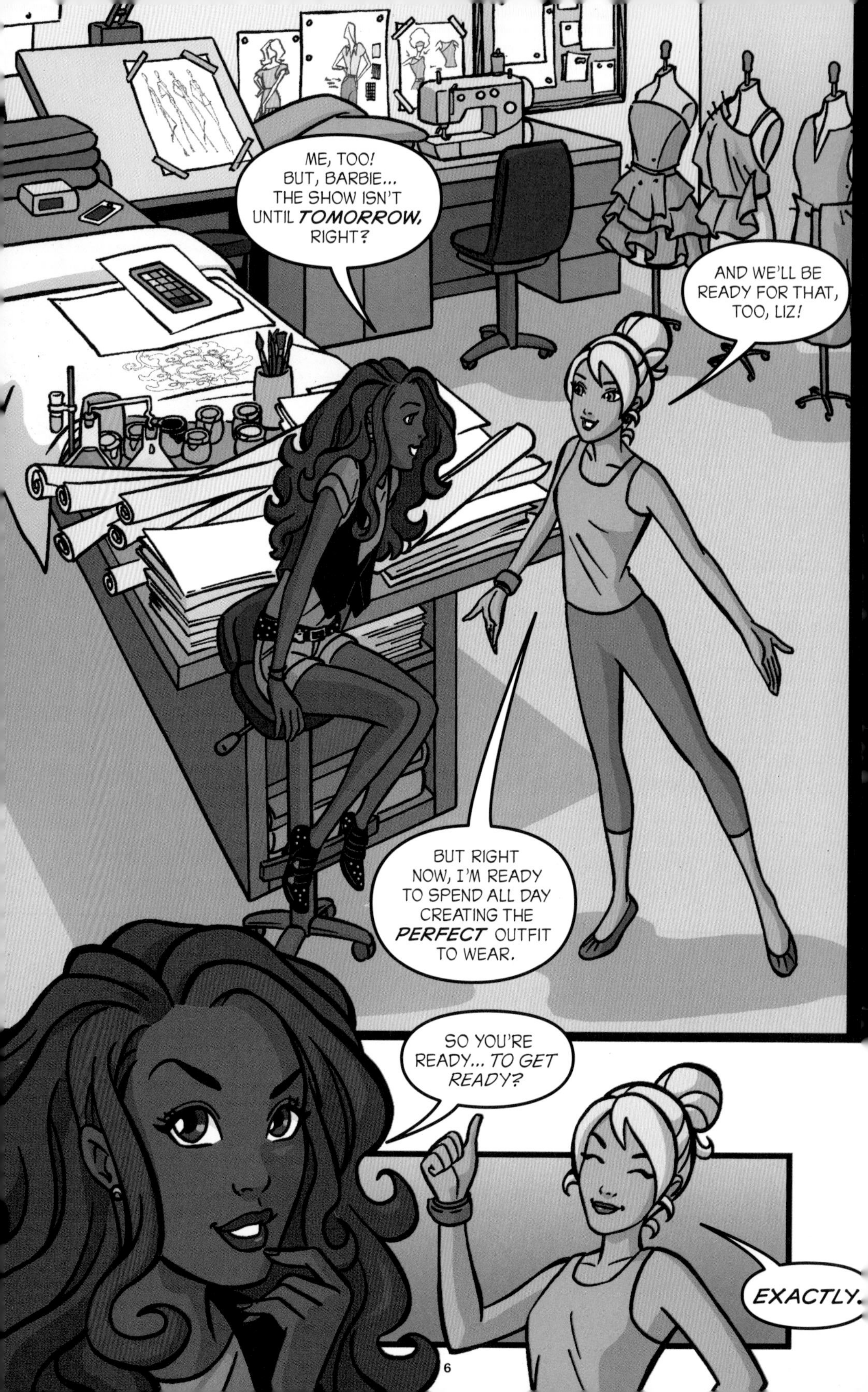
ME, TOO! BUT, BARBIE... THE SHOW ISN'T UNTIL TOMORROW, RIGHT?
AND WE'LL BE READY FOR THAT, TOO, LIZ!
BUT RIGHT NOW, I'M READY TO SPEND ALL DAY CREATING THE PERFECT OUTFIT TO WEAR.
SO YOU'RE READY... TO GET READY?
EXACTLY.

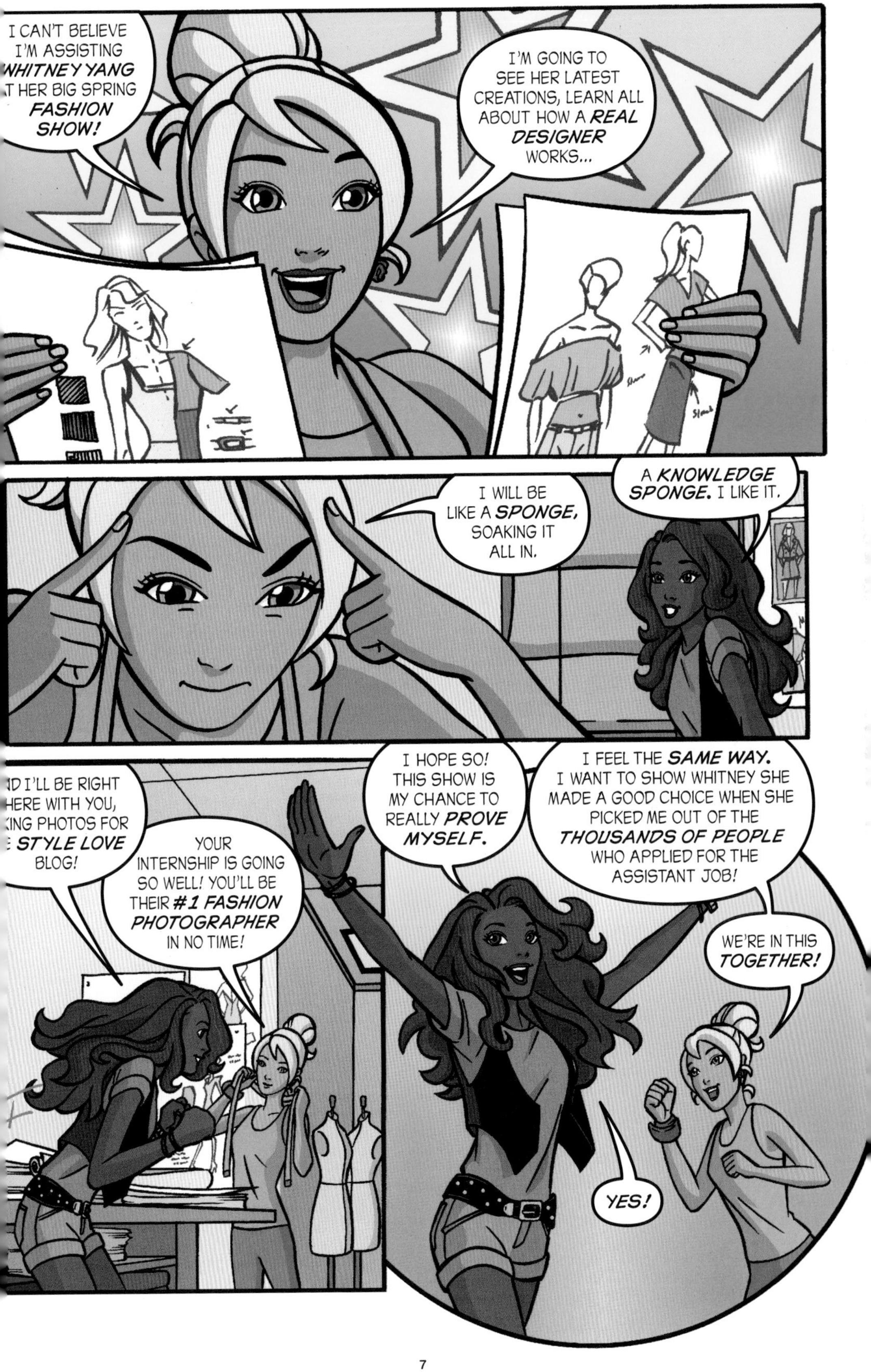
I CAN'T BELIEVE I'M ASSISTING WHITNEY YANG T HER BIG SPRING FASHION SHOW!
I'M GOING TO SEE HER LATEST CREATIONS, LEARN ALL ABOUT HOW A REAL DESIGNER WORKS...
I WILL BE LIKE A SPONGE, SOAKING IT ALL IN.
A KNOWLEDGE SPONGE. I LIKE IT.
D I'LL BE RIGHT HERE WITH YOU, KING PHOTOS FOR STYLE LOVE BLOG!
YOUR INTERNSHIP IS GOING SO WELL! YOU'LL BE THEIR #1 FASHION PHOTOGRAPHER IN NO TIME!
I HOPE SO! THIS SHOW IS MY CHANCE TO REALLY PROVE MYSELF.
I FEEL THE SAME WAY. I WANT TO SHOW WHITNEY SHE MADE A GOOD CHOICE WHEN SHE PICKED ME OUT OF THE THOUSANDS OF PEOPLE WHO APPLIED FOR THE ASSISTANT JOB!
WE'RE IN THIS TOGETHER!
YES!

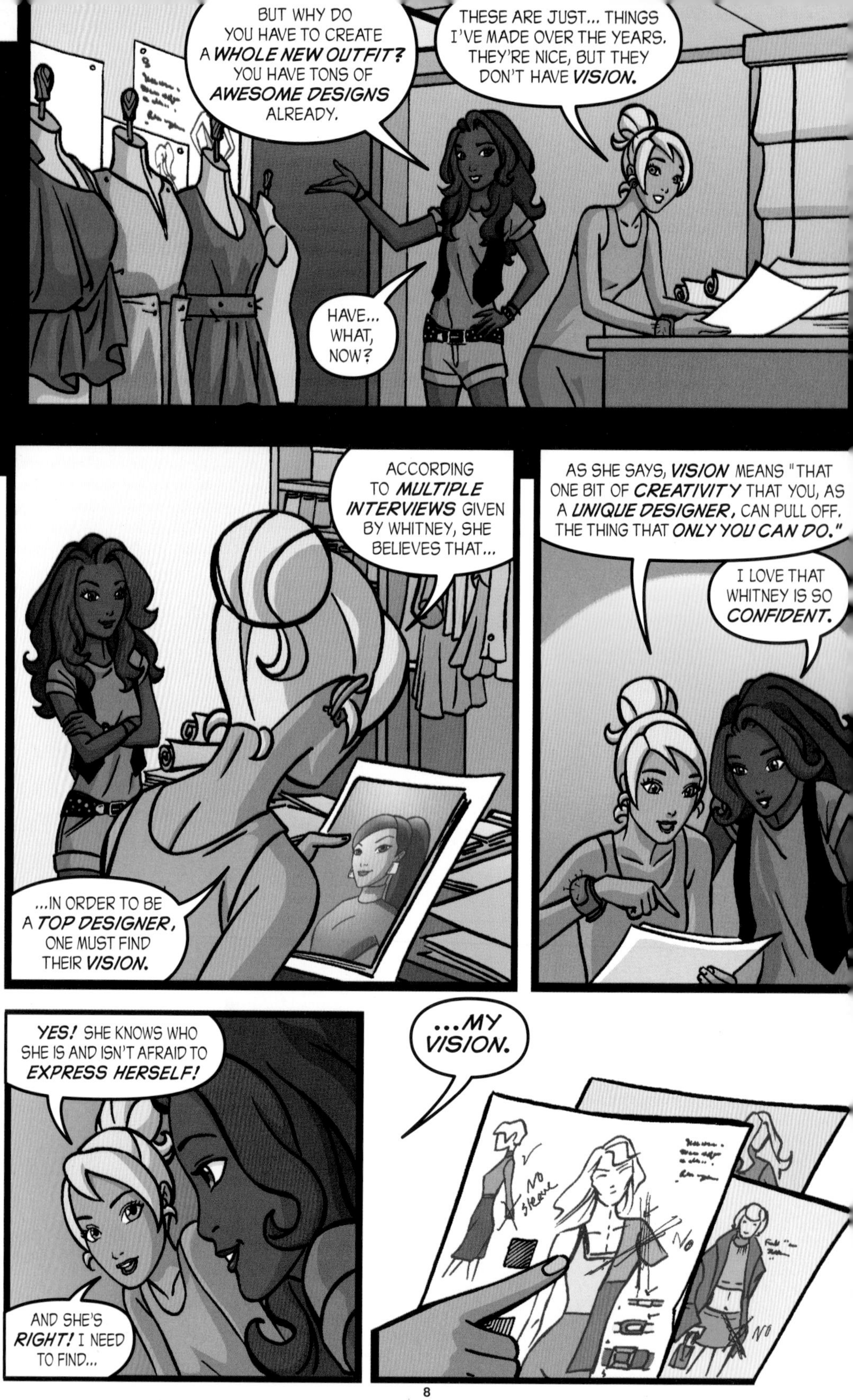
BUT WHY DO YOU HAVE TO CREATE A WHOLE NEW OUTFIT? YOU HAVE TONS OF AWESOME DESIGNS ALREADY.
THESE ARE JUST... THINGS I'VE MADE OVER THE YEARS. THEY'RE NICE, BUT THEY DON'T HAVE VISION.
HAVE... WHAT, NOW?
ACCORDING TO MULTIPLE INTERVIEWS GIVEN BY WHITNEY, SHE BELIEVES THAT...
...IN ORDER TO BE A TOP DESIGNER, ONE MUST FIND THEIR VISION.
AS SHE SAYS, VISION MEANS "THAT ONE BIT OF CREATIVITY THAT YOU, AS A UNIQUE DESIGNER, CAN PULL OFF. THE THING THAT ONLY YOU CAN DO."
I LOVE THAT WHITNEY IS SO CONFIDENT.
YES! SHE KNOWS WHO SHE IS AND ISN'T AFRAID TO EXPRESS HERSELF!
AND SHE'S RIGHT! I NEED TO FIND...
...MY VISION.

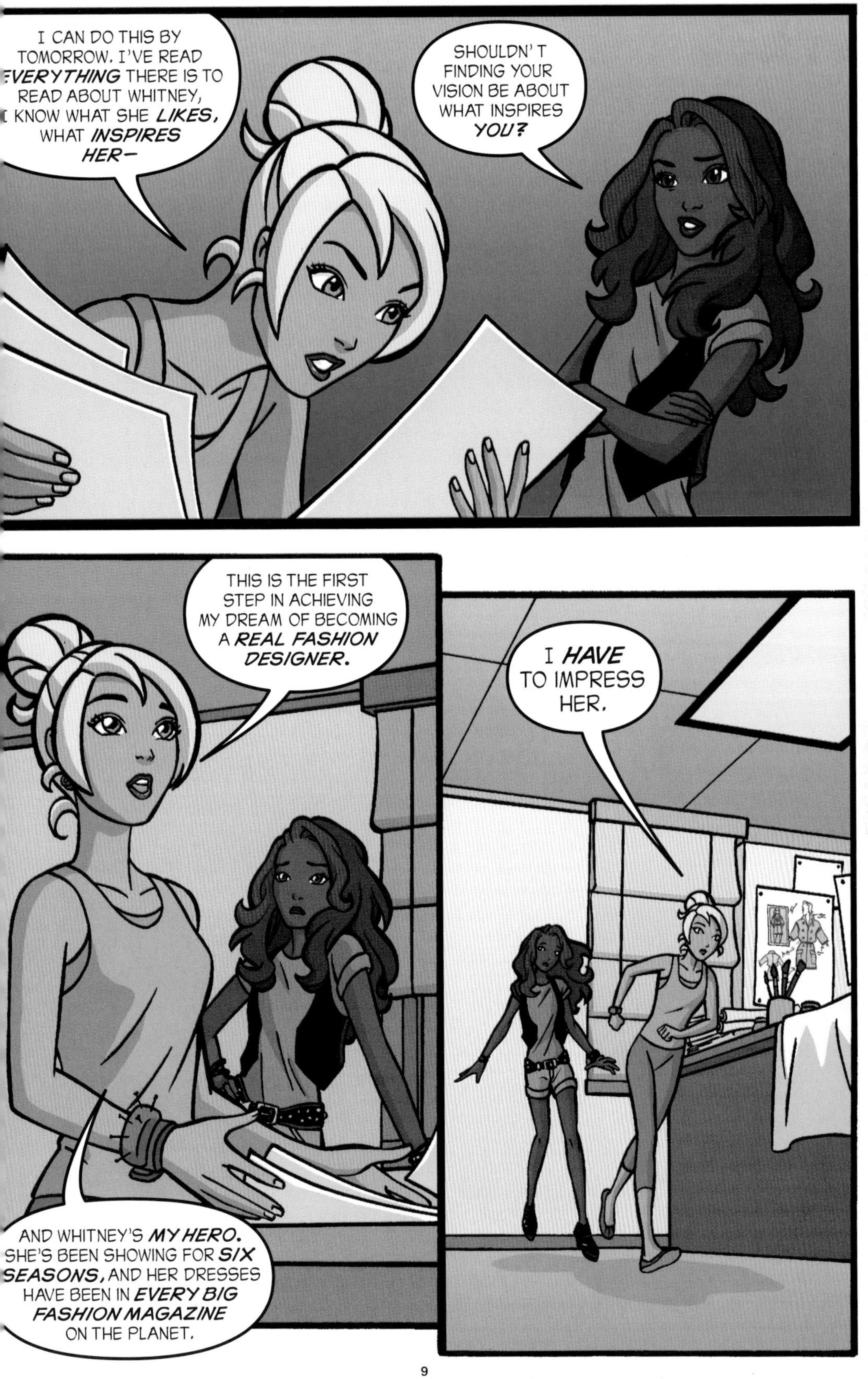
I CAN DO THIS BY TOMORROW. I'VE READ EVERYTHING THERE IS TO READ ABOUT WHITNEY, I KNOW WHAT SHE LIKES, WHAT INSPIRES HER—
SHOULDN'T FINDING YOUR VISION BE ABOUT WHAT INSPIRES YOU?
THIS IS THE FIRST STEP IN ACHIEVING MY DREAM OF BECOMING A REAL FASHION DESIGNER.
AND WHITNEY'S MY HERO. SHE'S BEEN SHOWING FOR SIX SEASONS, AND HER DRESSES HAVE BEEN IN EVERY BIG FASHION MAGAZINE ON THE PLANET.
I HAVE TO IMPRESS HER.

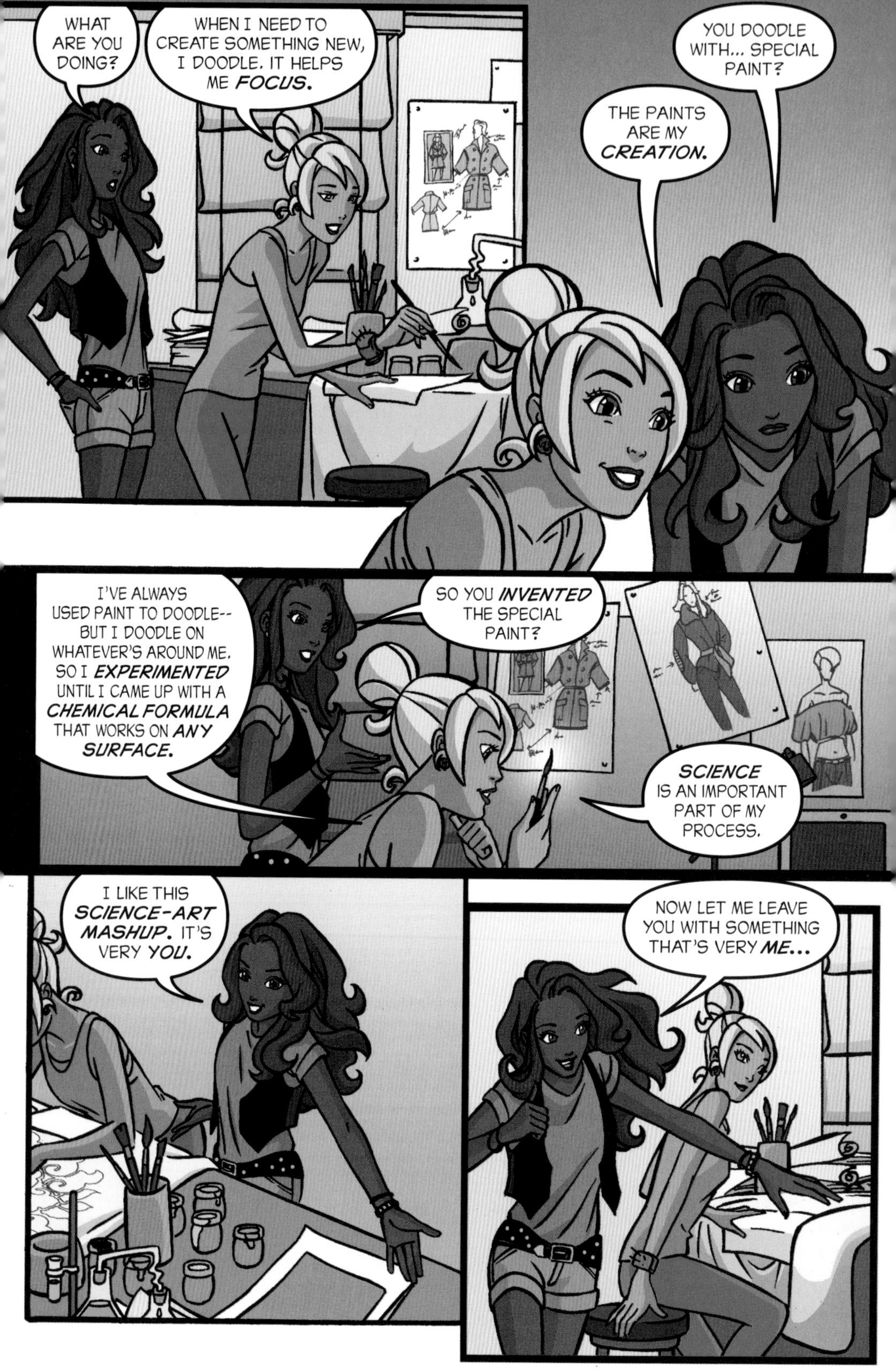
WHAT ARE YOU DOING?
WHEN I NEED TO CREATE SOMETHING NEW, I DOODLE. IT HELPS ME FOCUS.
YOU DOODLE WITH... SPECIAL PAINT?
THE PAINTS ARE MY CREATION.
I'VE ALWAYS USED PAINT TO DOODLE-- BUT I DOODLE ON WHATEVER'S AROUND ME. SO I EXPERIMENTED UNTIL I CAME UP WITH A CHEMICAL FORMULA THAT WORKS ON ANY SURFACE.
SO YOU INVENTED THE SPECIAL PAINT?
SCIENCE IS AN IMPORTANT PART OF MY PROCESS.
I LIKE THIS SCIENCE-ART MASHUP. IT'S VERY YOU.
NOW LET ME LEAVE YOU WITH SOMETHING THAT'S VERY ME...

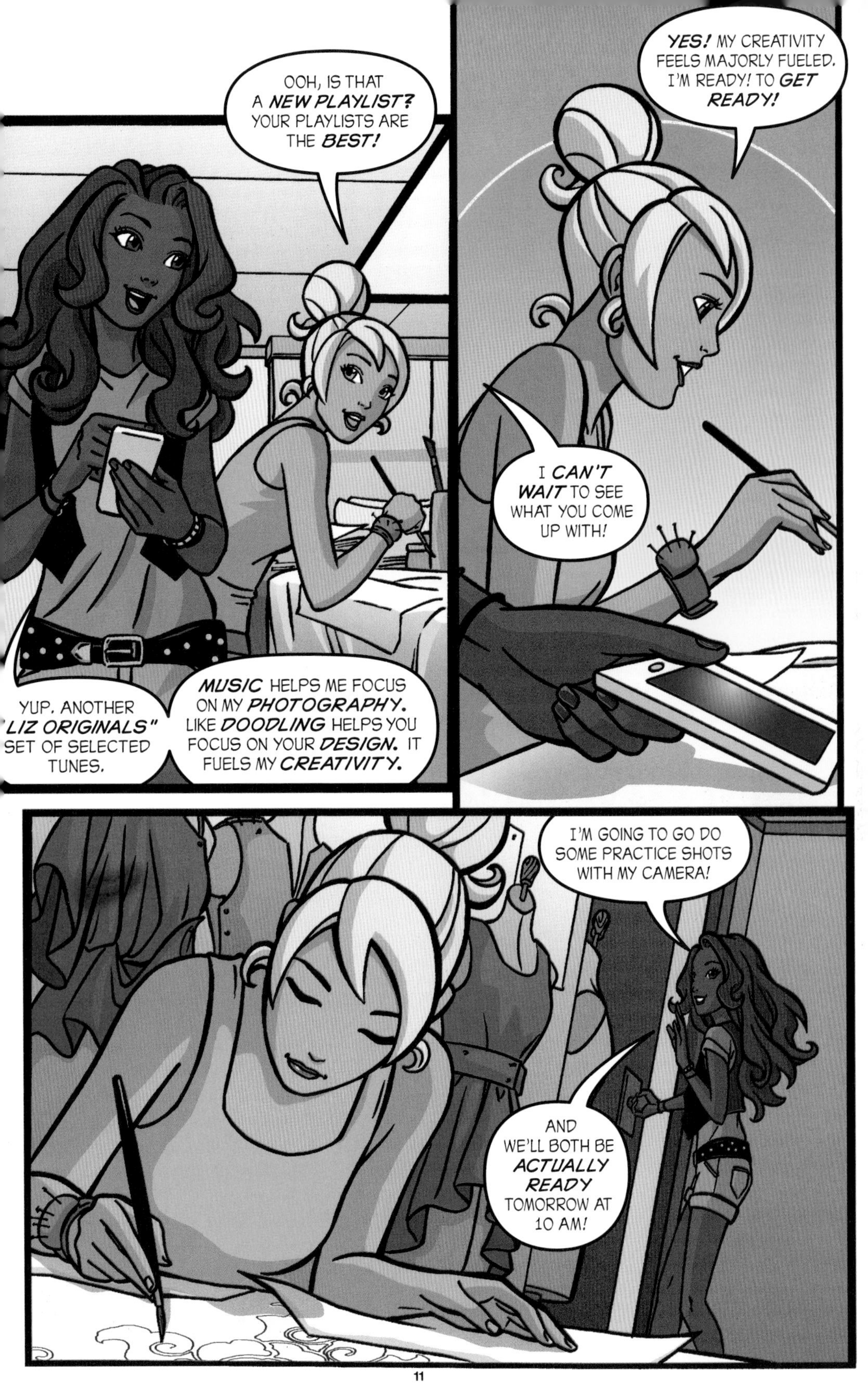
OOH, IS THAT A NEW PLAYLIST? YOUR PLAYLISTS ARE THE BEST!
YUP. ANOTHER "LIZ ORIGINALS" SET OF SELECTED TUNES.
MUSIC HELPS ME FOCUS ON MY PHOTOGRAPHY. LIKE DOODLING HELPS YOU FOCUS ON YOUR DESIGN. IT FUELS MY CREATIVITY.
YES! MY CREATIVITY FEELS MAJORLY FUELED. I'M READY! TO GET READY!
I CAN'T WAIT TO SEE WHAT YOU COME UP WITH!
I'M GOING TO GO DO SOME PRACTICE SHOTS WITH MY CAMERA!
AND WE'LL BOTH BE ACTUALLY READY TOMORROW AT 10 AM!

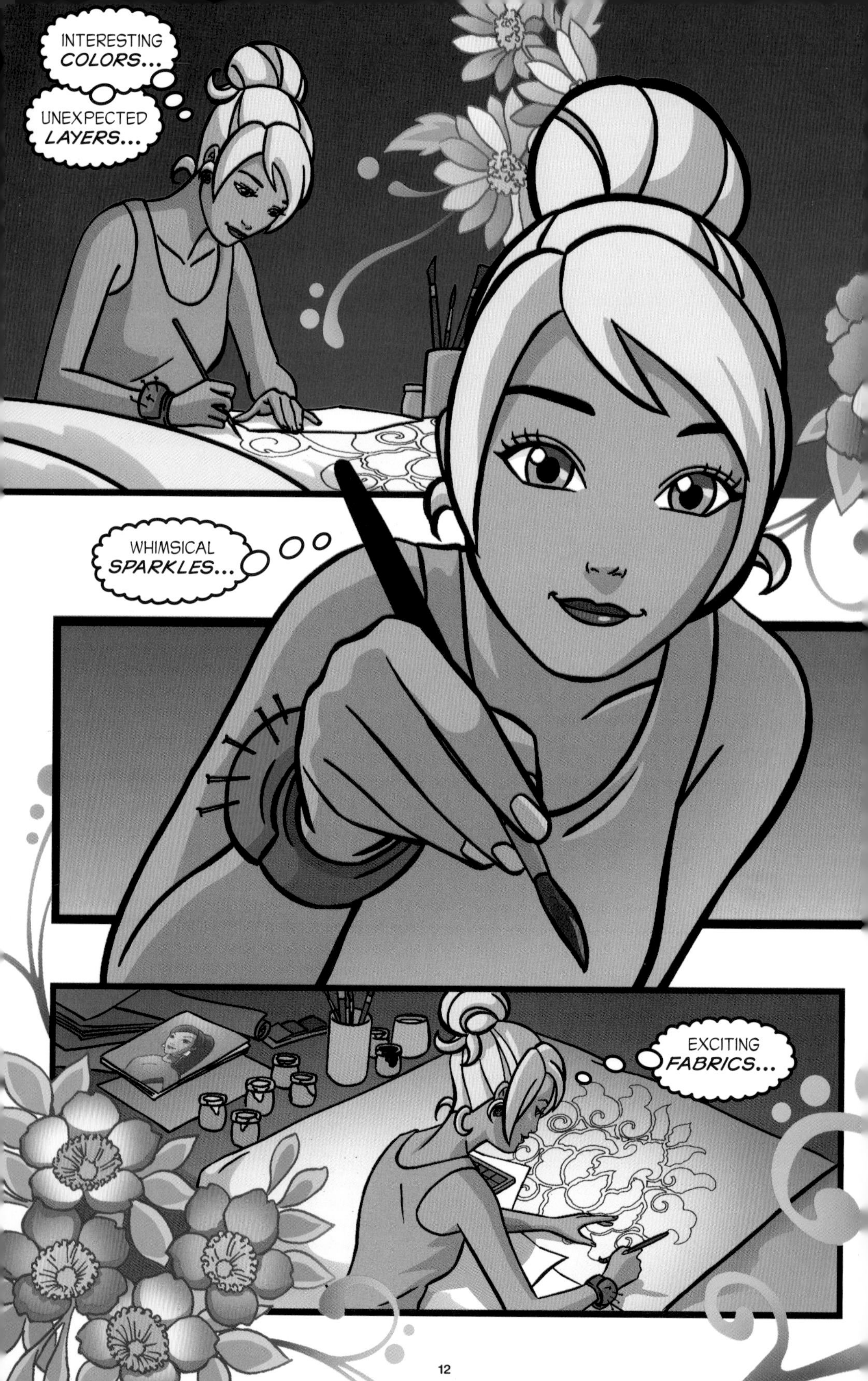
INTERESTING COLORS...
UNEXPECTED LAYERS...
WHIMSICAL SPARKLES...
EXCITING FABRICS...

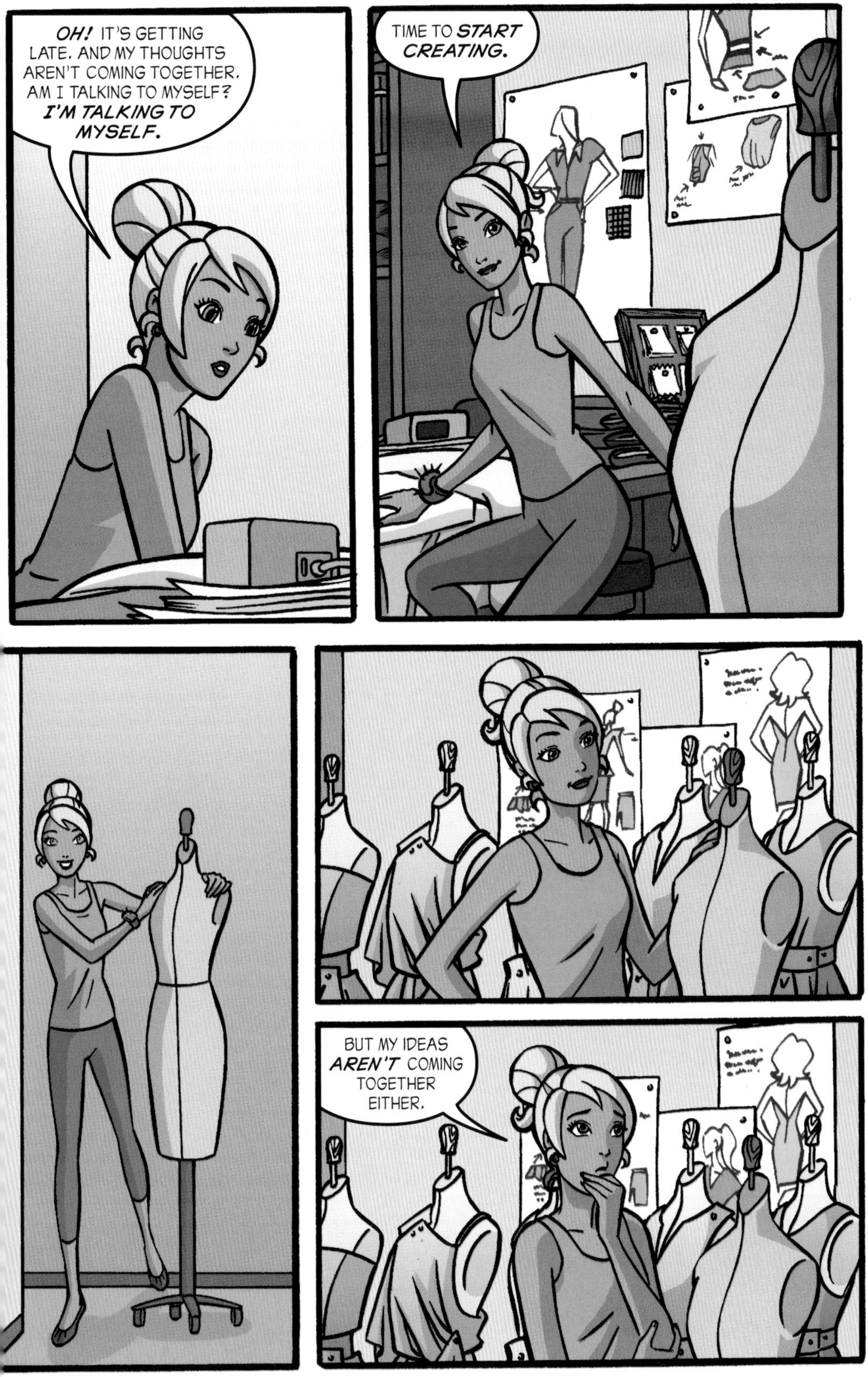

OH! IT'S GETTING LATE. AND MY THOUGHTS AREN'T COMING TOGETHER. AM I TALKING TO MYSELF? I'M TALKING TO MYSELF.
TIME TO START CREATING.
BUT MY IDEAS AREN'T COMING TOGETHER EITHER.

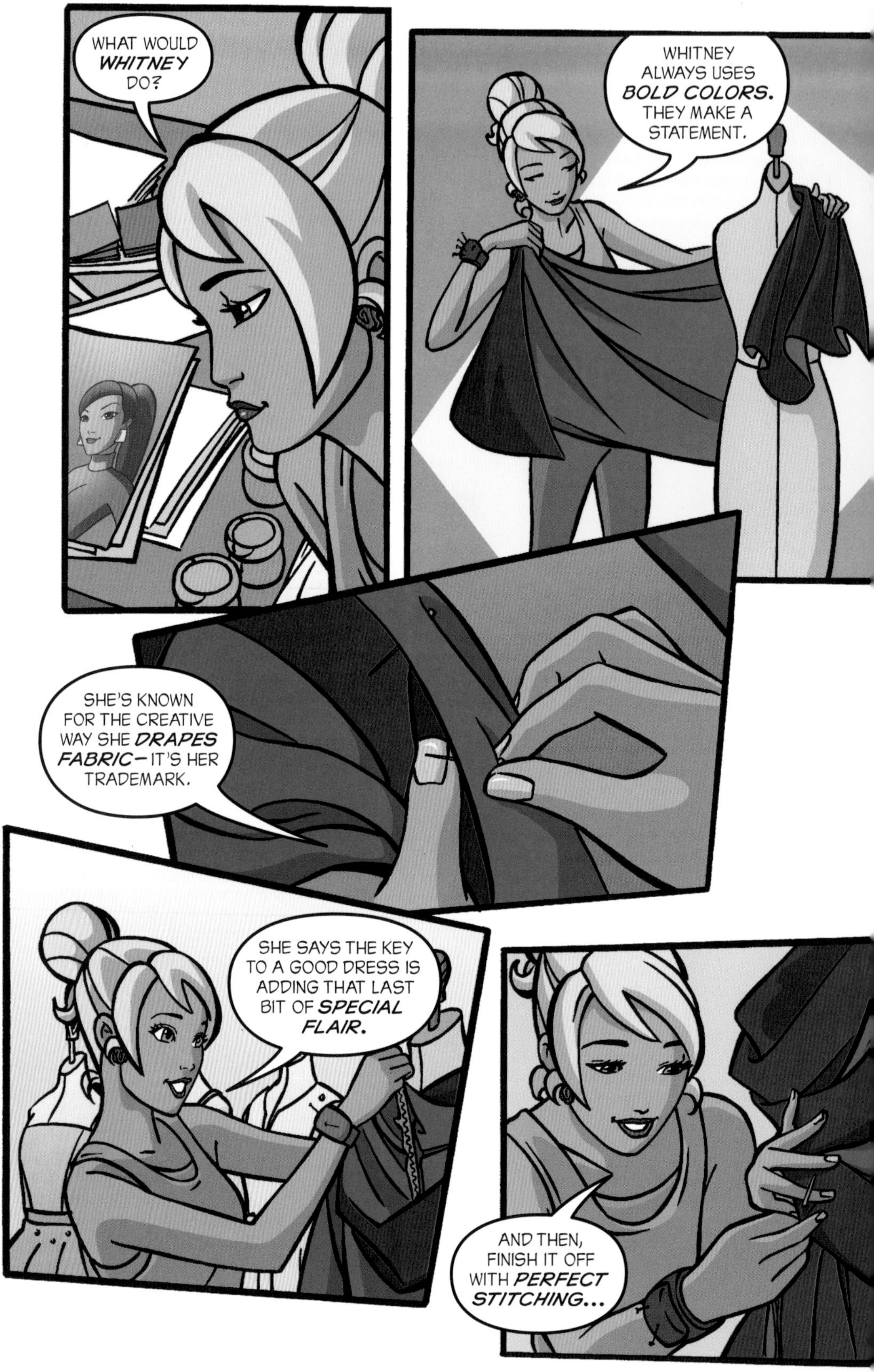
WHAT WOULD WHITNEY DO?
WHITNEY ALWAYS USES BOLD COLORS. THEY MAKE A STATEMENT.
SHE'S KNOWN FOR THE CREATIVE WAY SHE DRAPES FABRIC– IT'S HER TRADEMARK.
SHE SAYS THE KEY TO A GOOD DRESS IS ADDING THAT LAST BIT OF SPECIAL FLAIR.
AND THEN, FINISH IT OFF WITH PERFECT STITCHING...

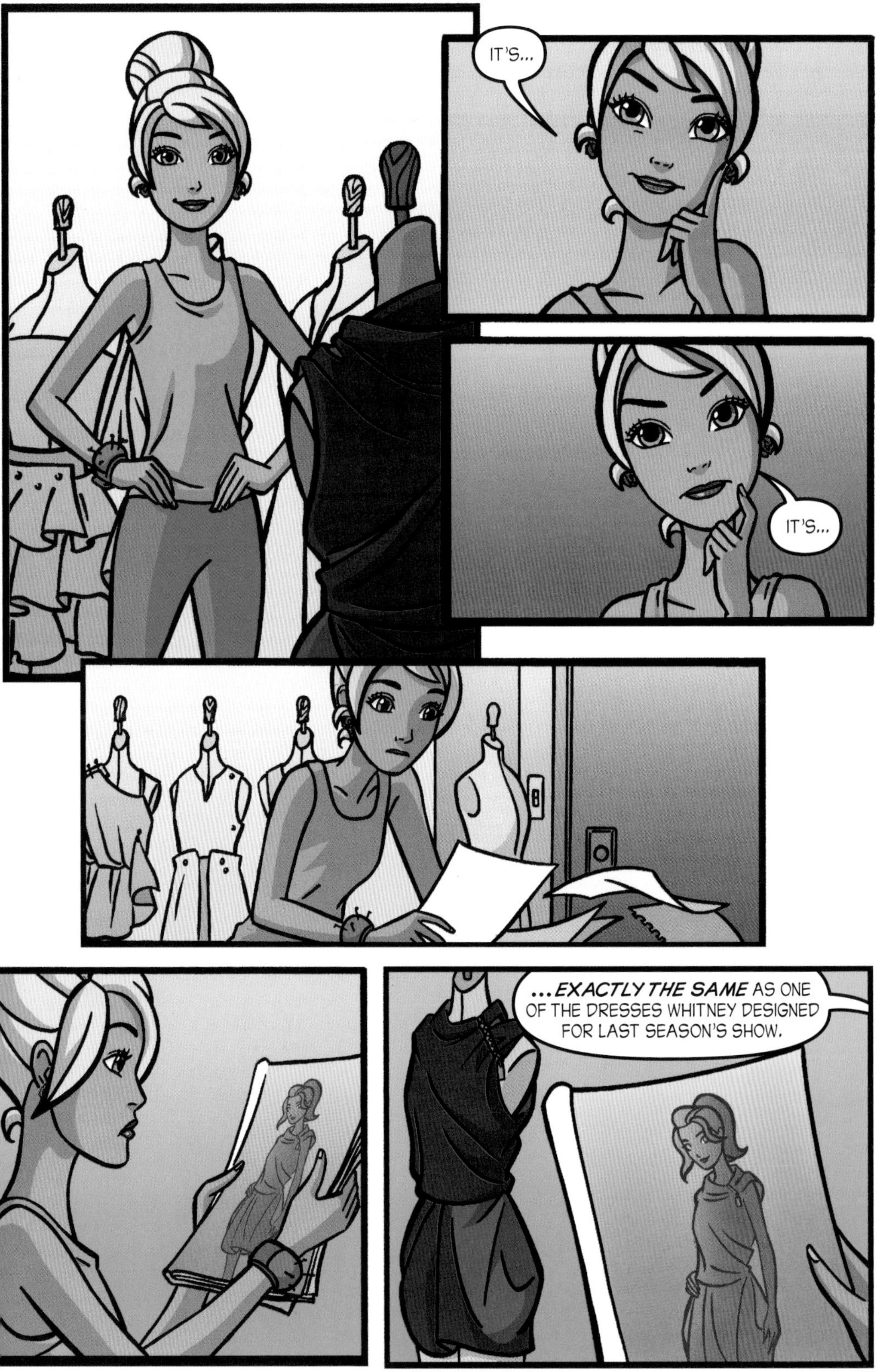
IT'S...
IT'S...
...EXACTLY THE SAME AS ONE OF THE DRESSES WHITNEY DESIGNED FOR LAST SEASON'S SHOW.

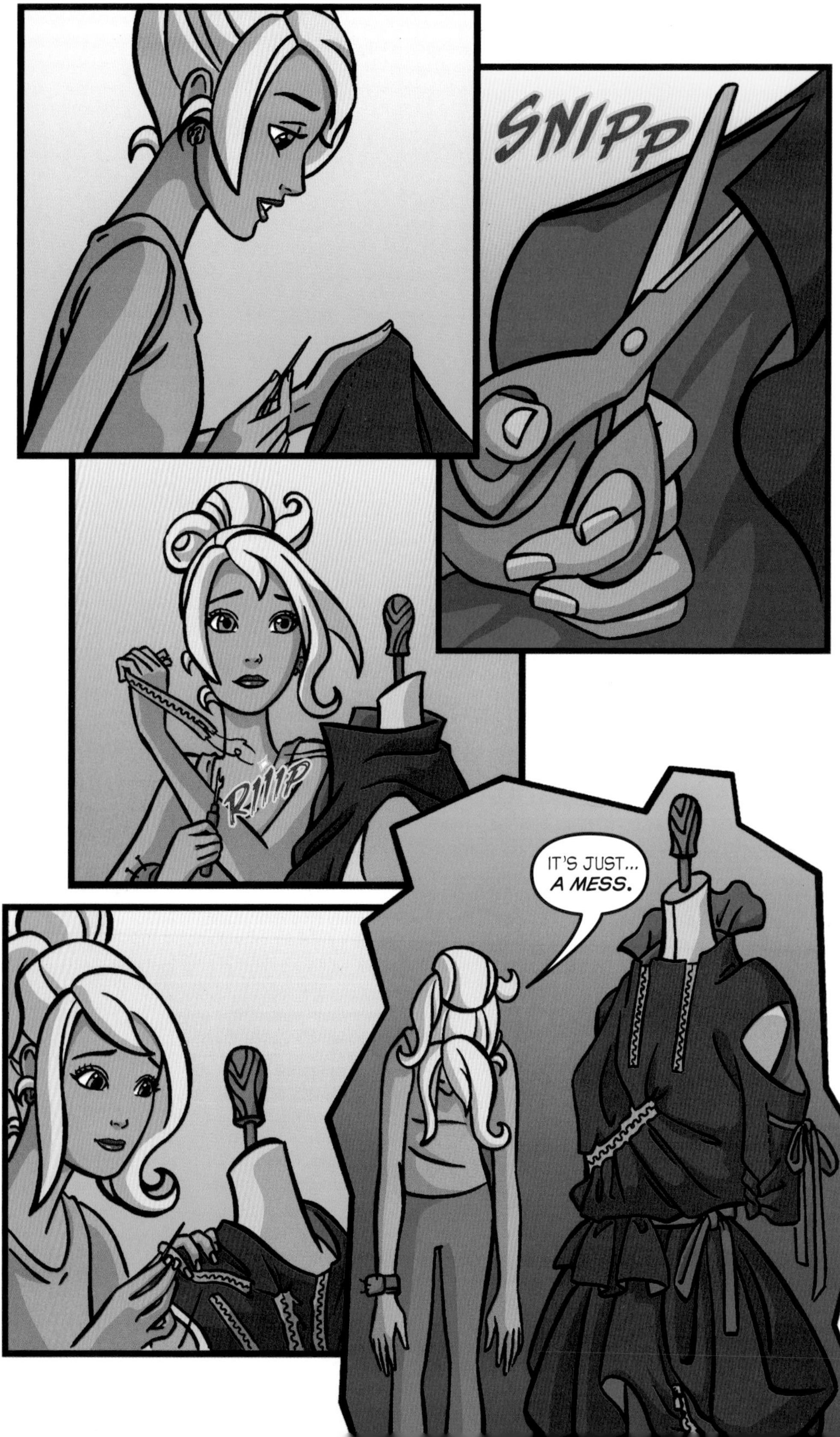
SNIPP
RIIIP
IT'S JUST... A MESS.

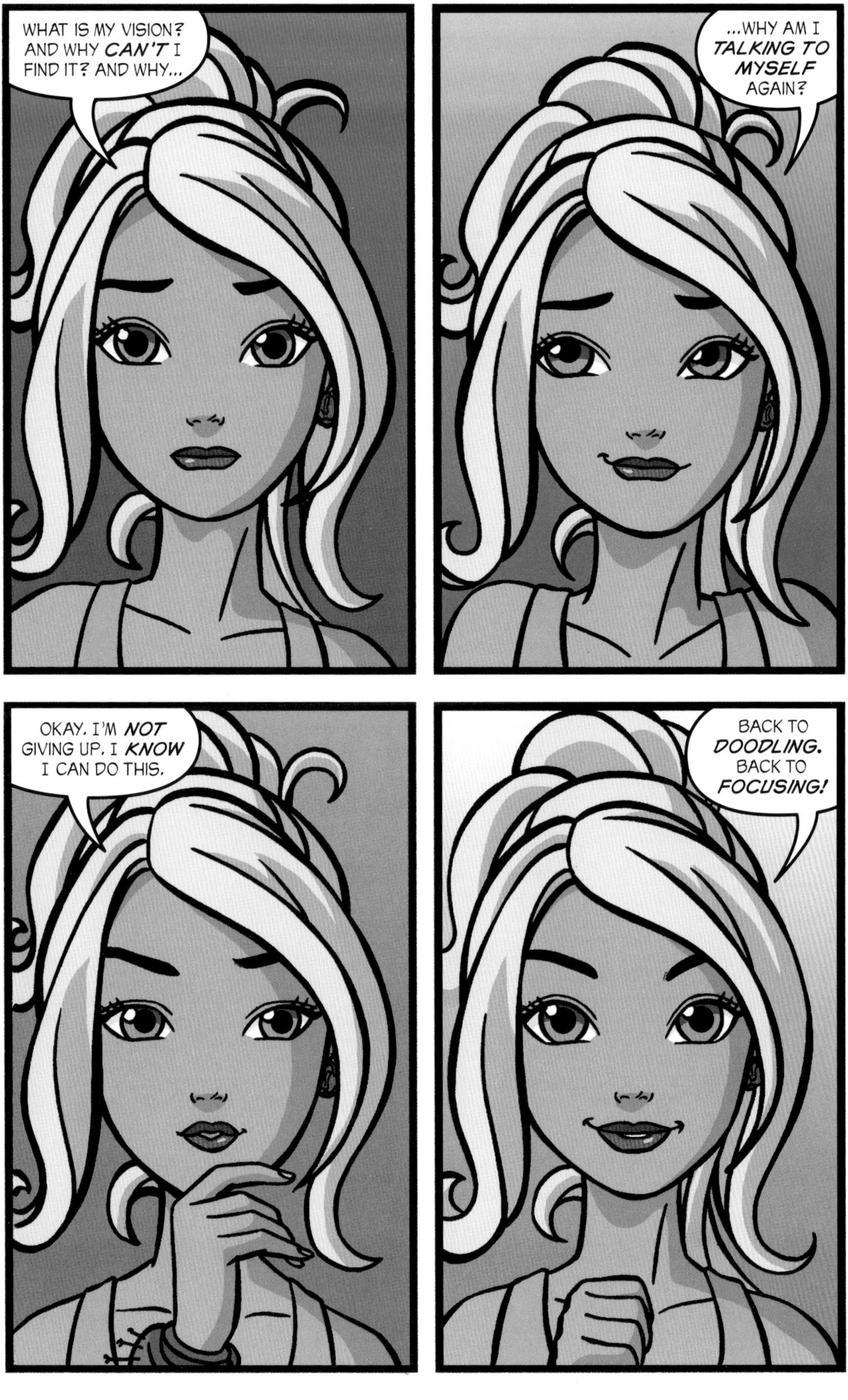
WHAT IS MY VISION? AND WHY CAN'T I FIND IT? AND WHY...
...WHY AM I TALKING TO MYSELF AGAIN?
OKAY. I'M NOT GIVING UP. I KNOW I CAN DO THIS.
BACK TO DOODLING. BACK TO FOCUSING!

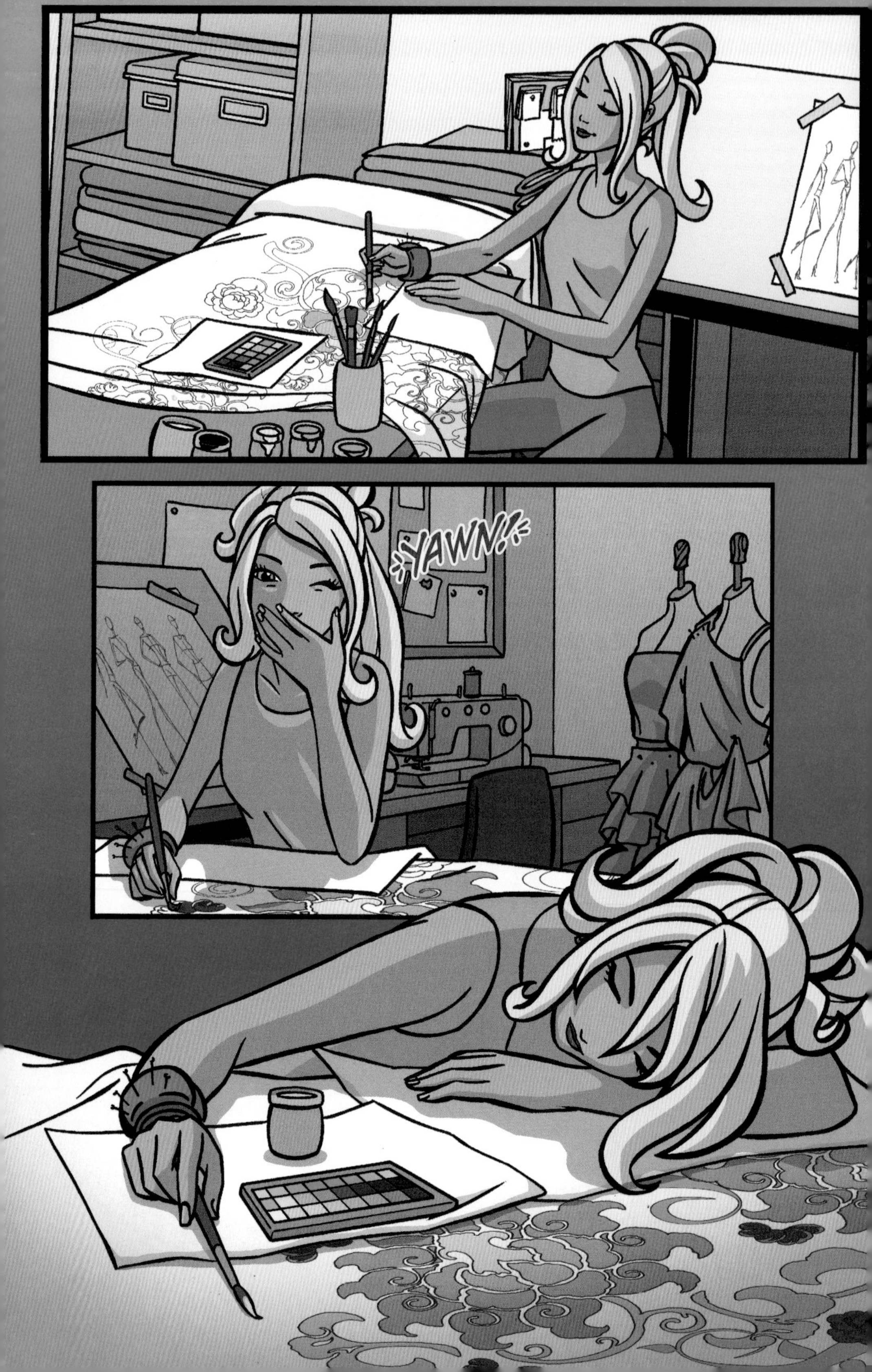
YAWN!

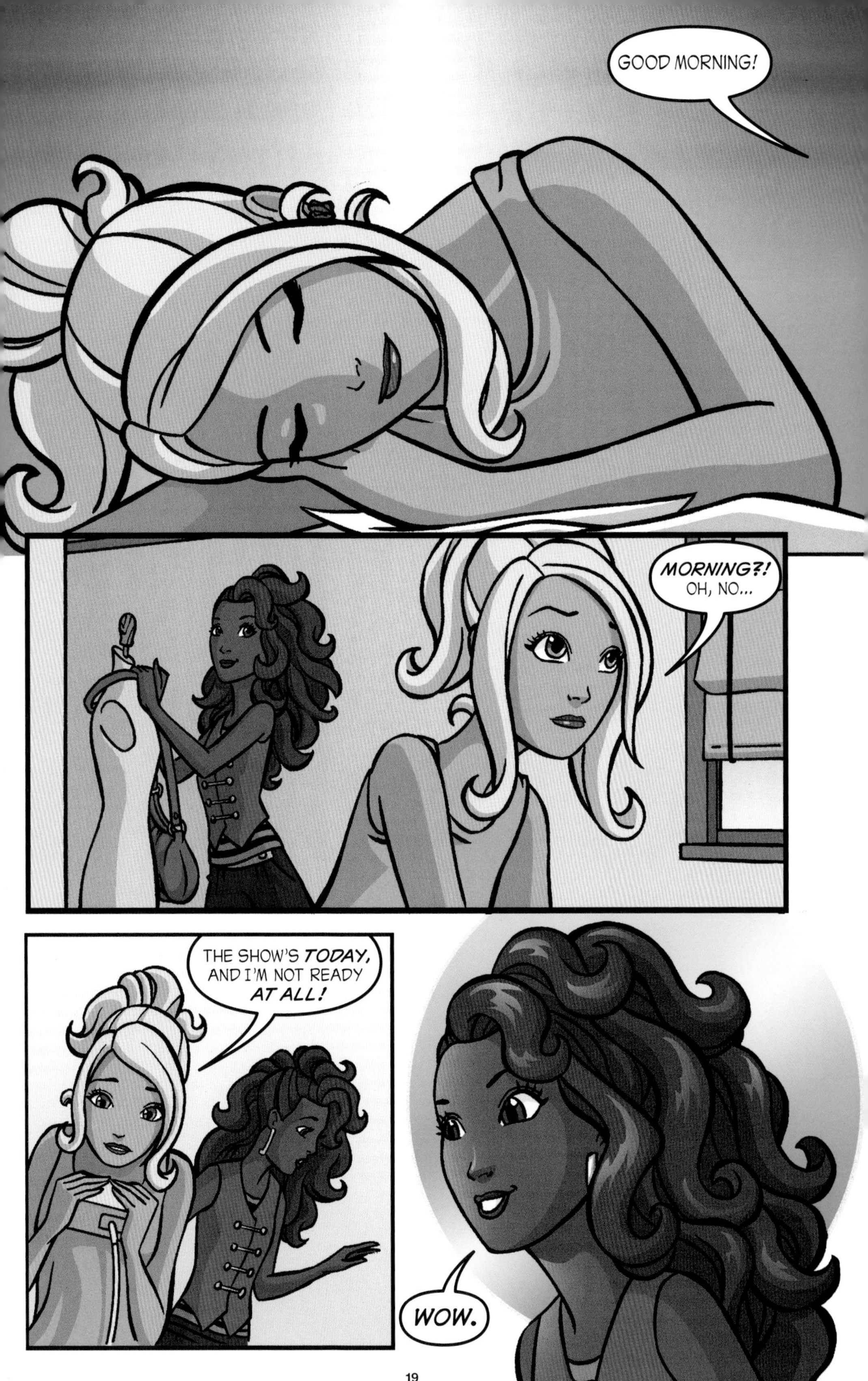
GOOD MORNING!
MORNING?! OH, NO...
THE SHOW'S TODAY, AND I'M NOT READY AT ALL!
WOW.

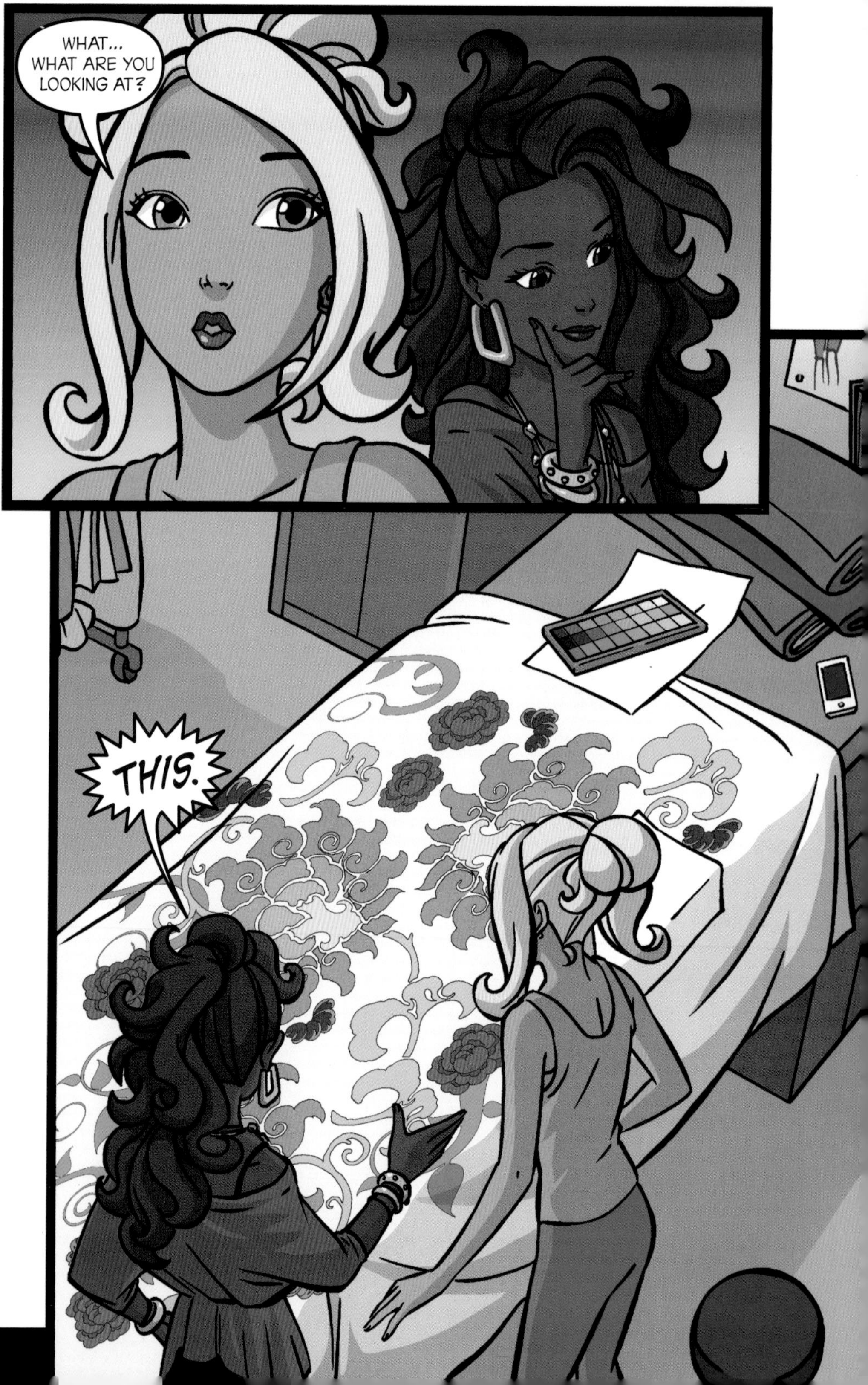
WHAT... WHAT ARE YOU LOOKING AT?
THIS.

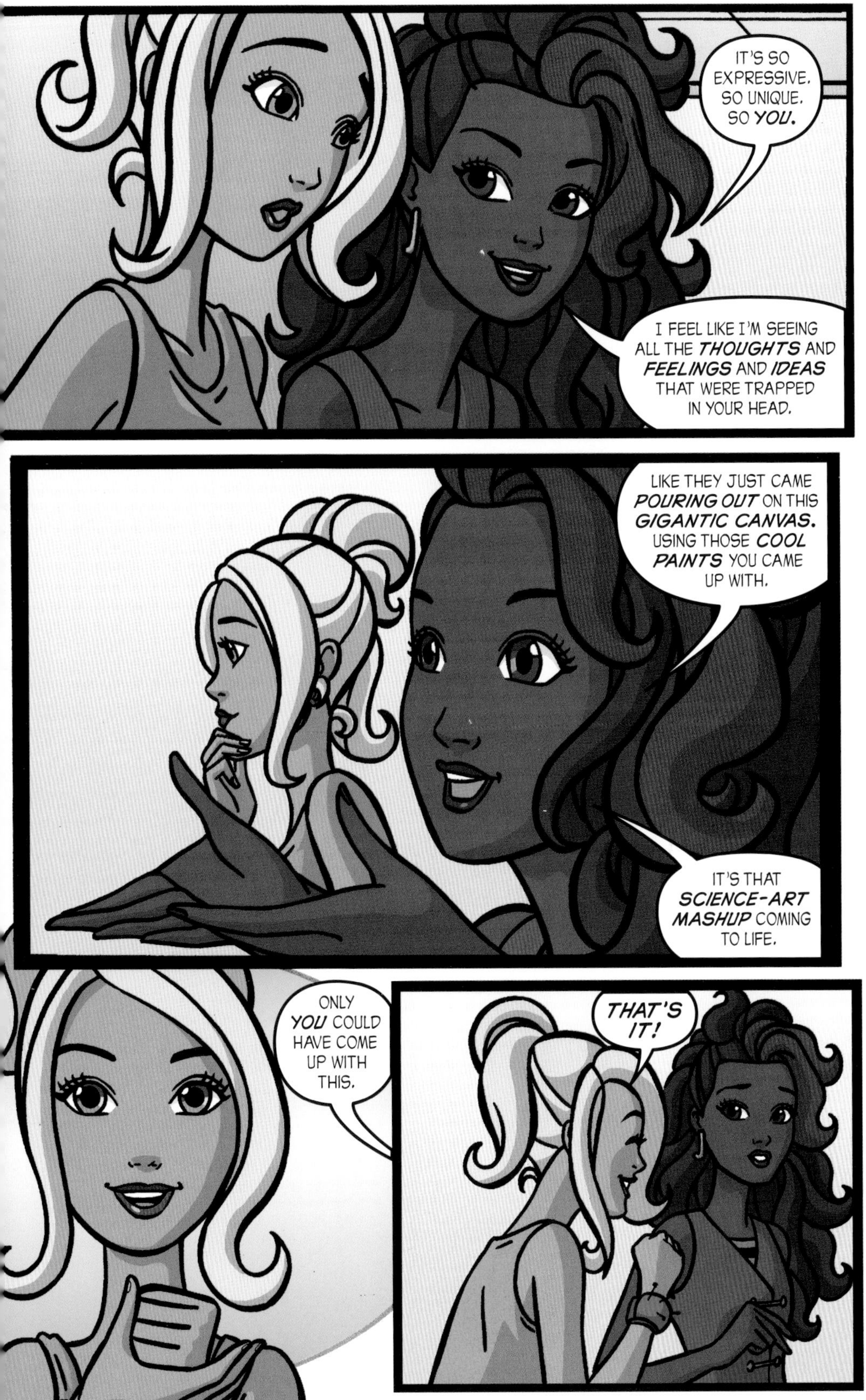
IT'S SO EXPRESSIVE. SO UNIQUE. SO YOU.
I FEEL LIKE I'M SEEING ALL THE THOUGHTS AND FEELINGS AND IDEAS THAT WERE TRAPPED IN YOUR HEAD.
LIKE THEY JUST CAME POURING OUT ON THIS GIGANTIC CANVAS. USING THOSE COOL PAINTS YOU CAME UP WITH.
IT'S THAT SCIENCE-ART MASHUP COMING TO LIFE.
ONLY YOU COULD HAVE COME UP WITH THIS.
THAT'S IT!

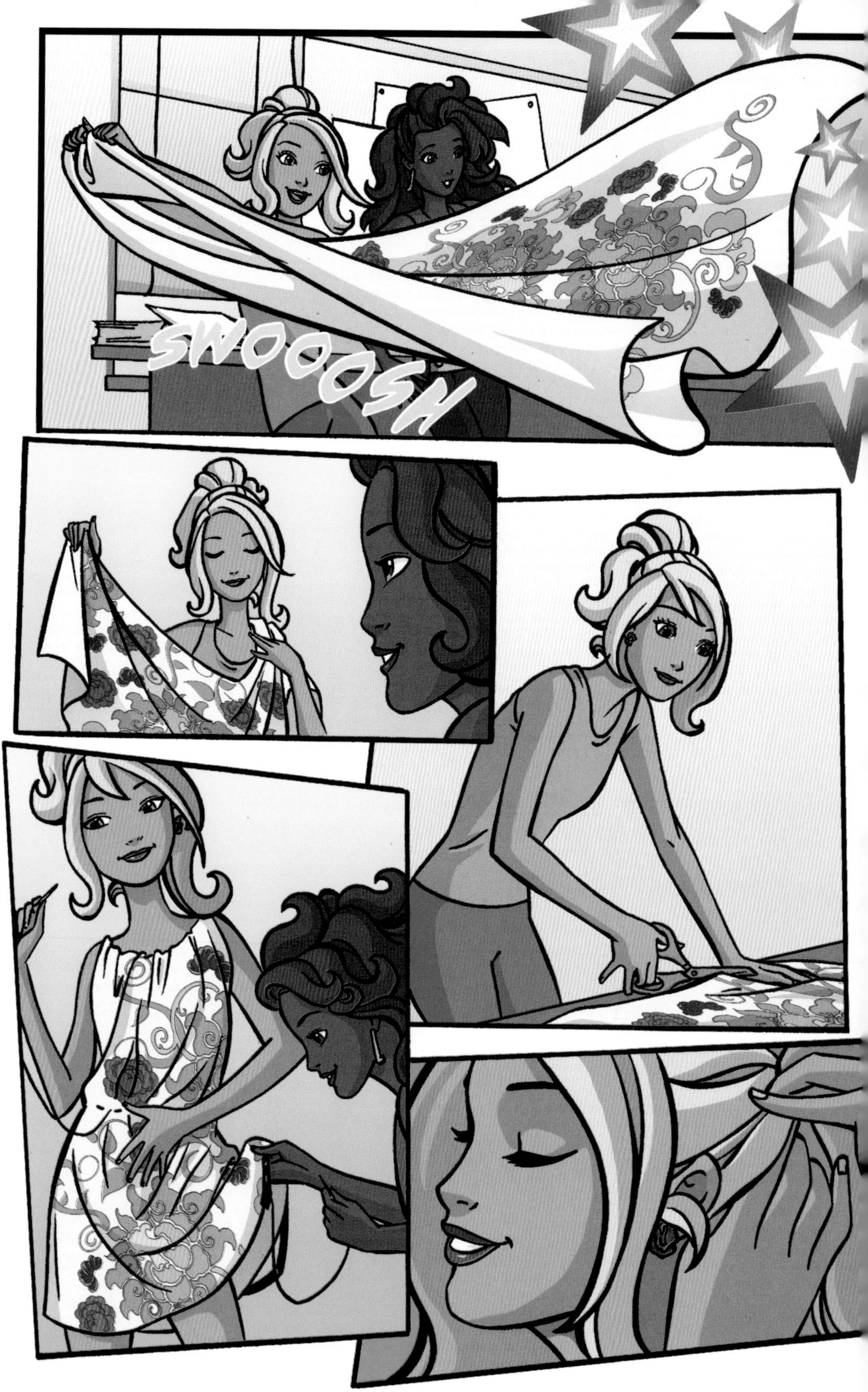
SWOOOSH

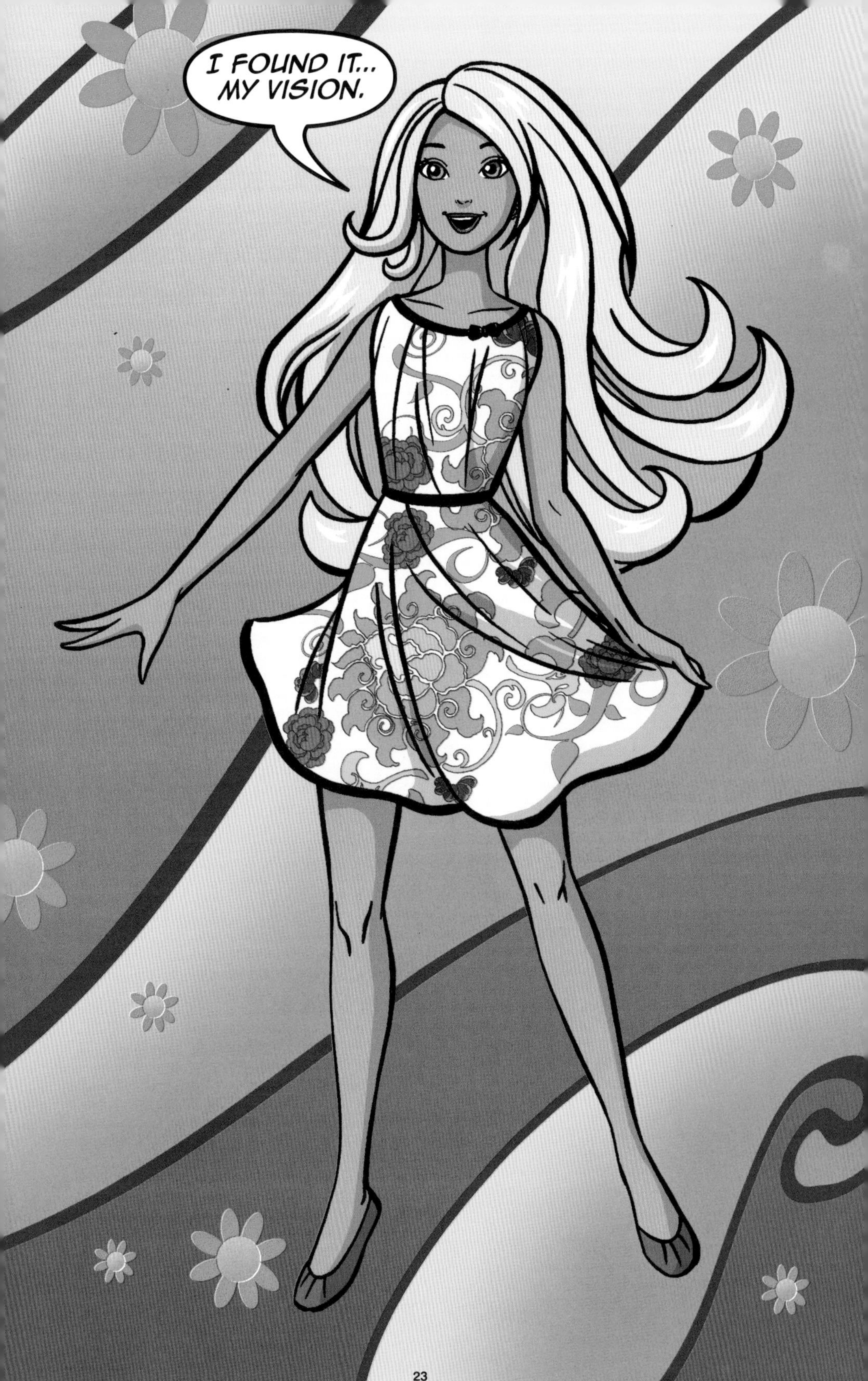
I FOUND IT... MY VISION.

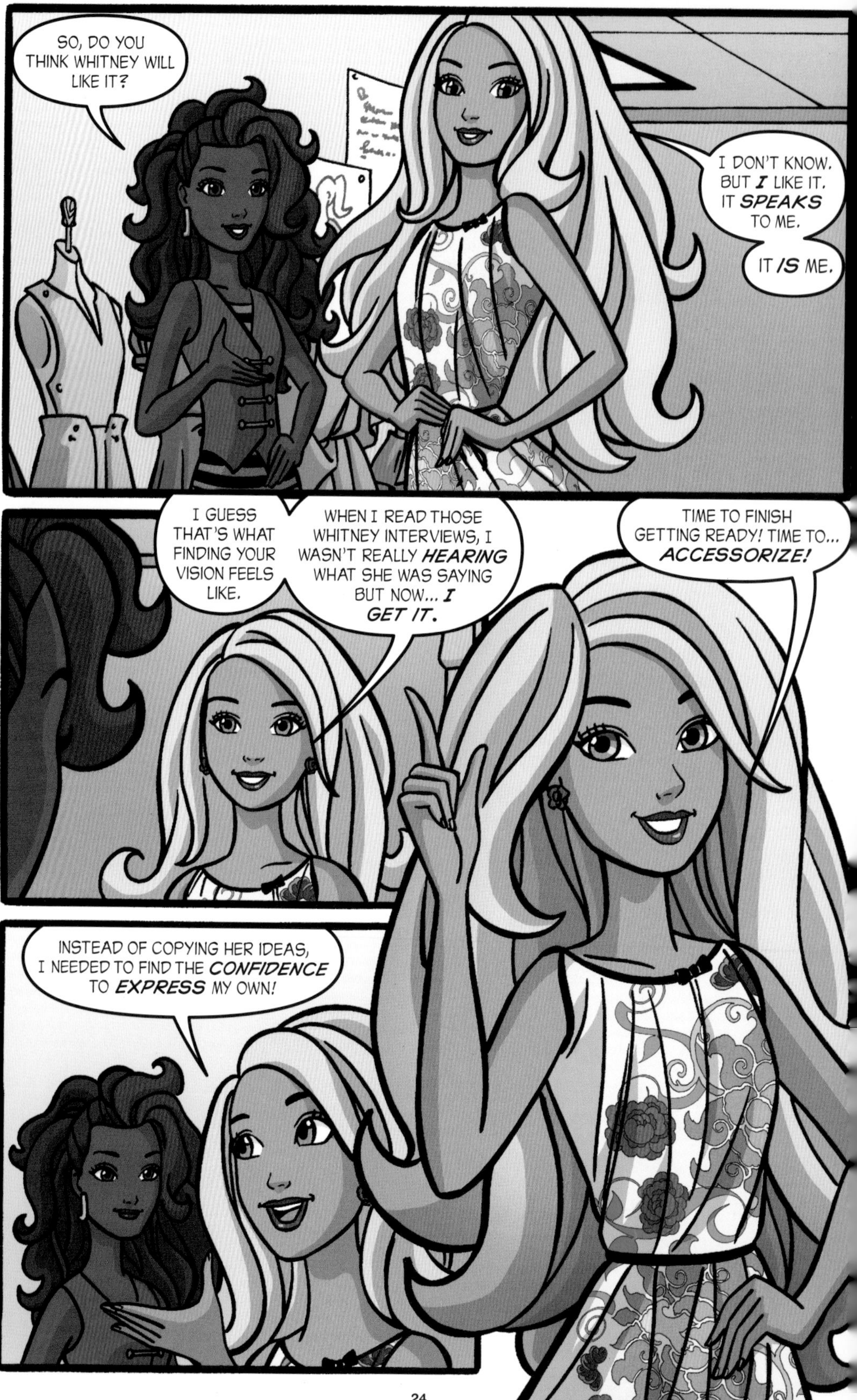
SO, DO YOU THINK WHITNEY WILL LIKE IT?
I DON'T KNOW. BUT *I* LIKE IT. IT *SPEAKS* TO ME.
IT *IS* ME.
I GUESS THAT'S WHAT FINDING YOUR VISION FEELS LIKE.
WHEN I READ THOSE WHITNEY INTERVIEWS, I WASN'T REALLY *HEARING* WHAT SHE WAS SAYING BUT NOW... *I GET IT*.
TIME TO FINISH GETTING READY! TIME TO... *ACCESSORIZE!*
INSTEAD OF COPYING HER IDEAS, I NEEDED TO FIND THE *CONFIDENCE* TO *EXPRESS* MY OWN!

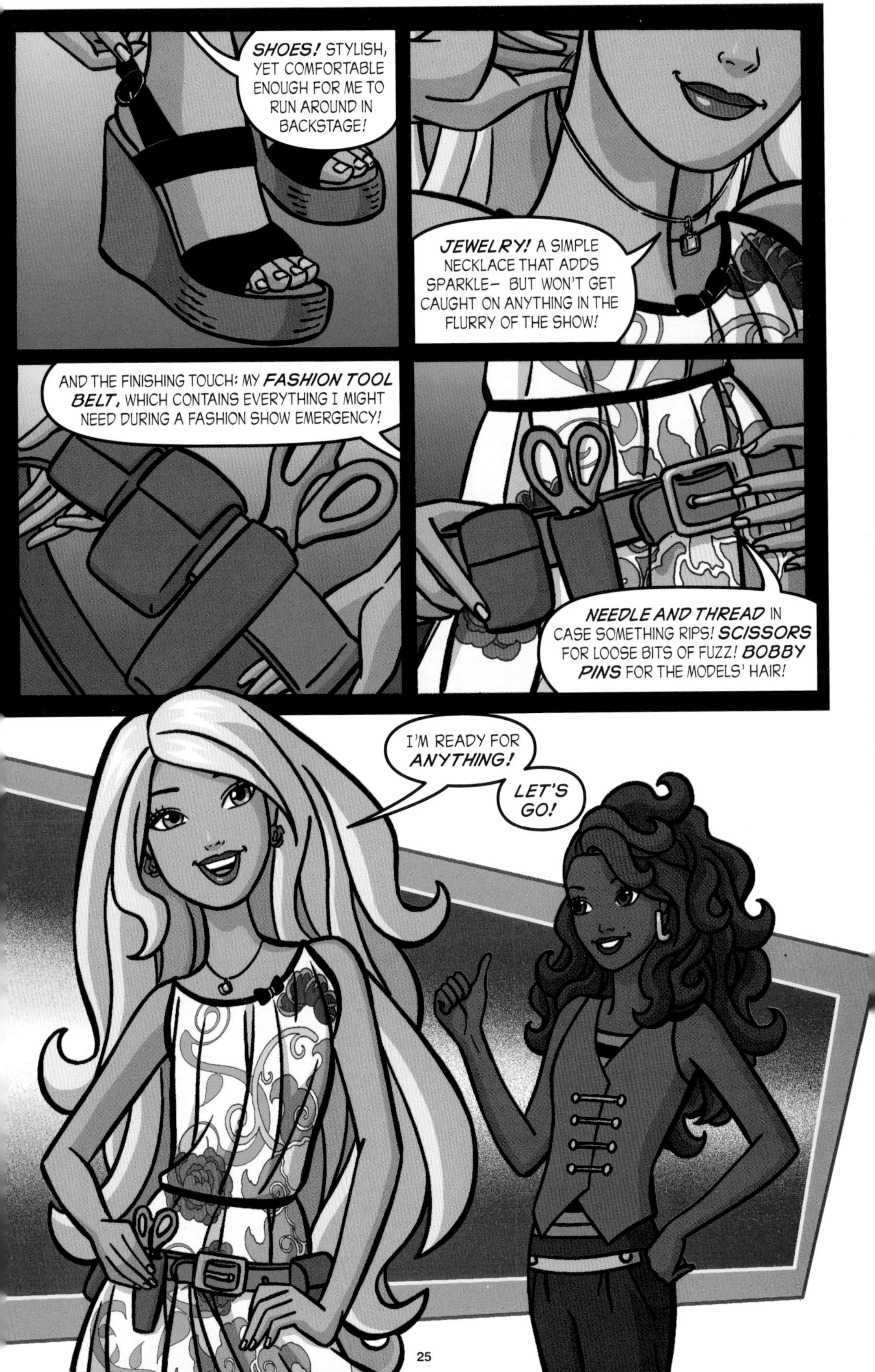
SHOES! STYLISH, YET COMFORTABLE ENOUGH FOR ME TO RUN AROUND IN BACKSTAGE!
JEWELRY! A SIMPLE NECKLACE THAT ADDS SPARKLE– BUT WON'T GET CAUGHT ON ANYTHING IN THE FLURRY OF THE SHOW!
AND THE FINISHING TOUCH: MY FASHION TOOL BELT, WHICH CONTAINS EVERYTHING I MIGHT NEED DURING A FASHION SHOW EMERGENCY!
NEEDLE AND THREAD IN CASE SOMETHING RIPS! SCISSORS FOR LOOSE BITS OF FUZZ! BOBBY PINS FOR THE MODELS' HAIR!
I'M READY FOR ANYTHING!
LET'S GO!

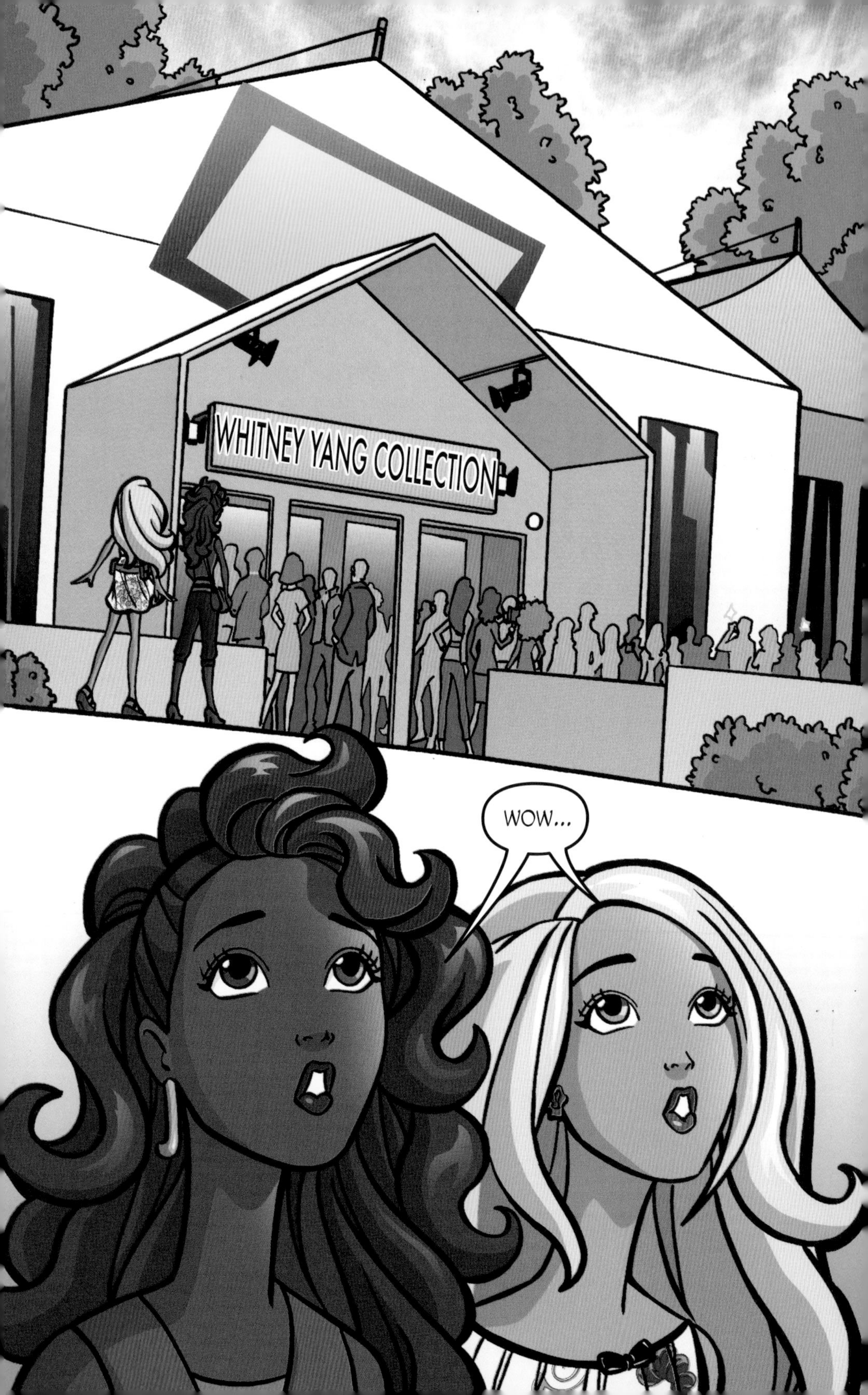
WHITNEY YANG COLLECTION
WOW...

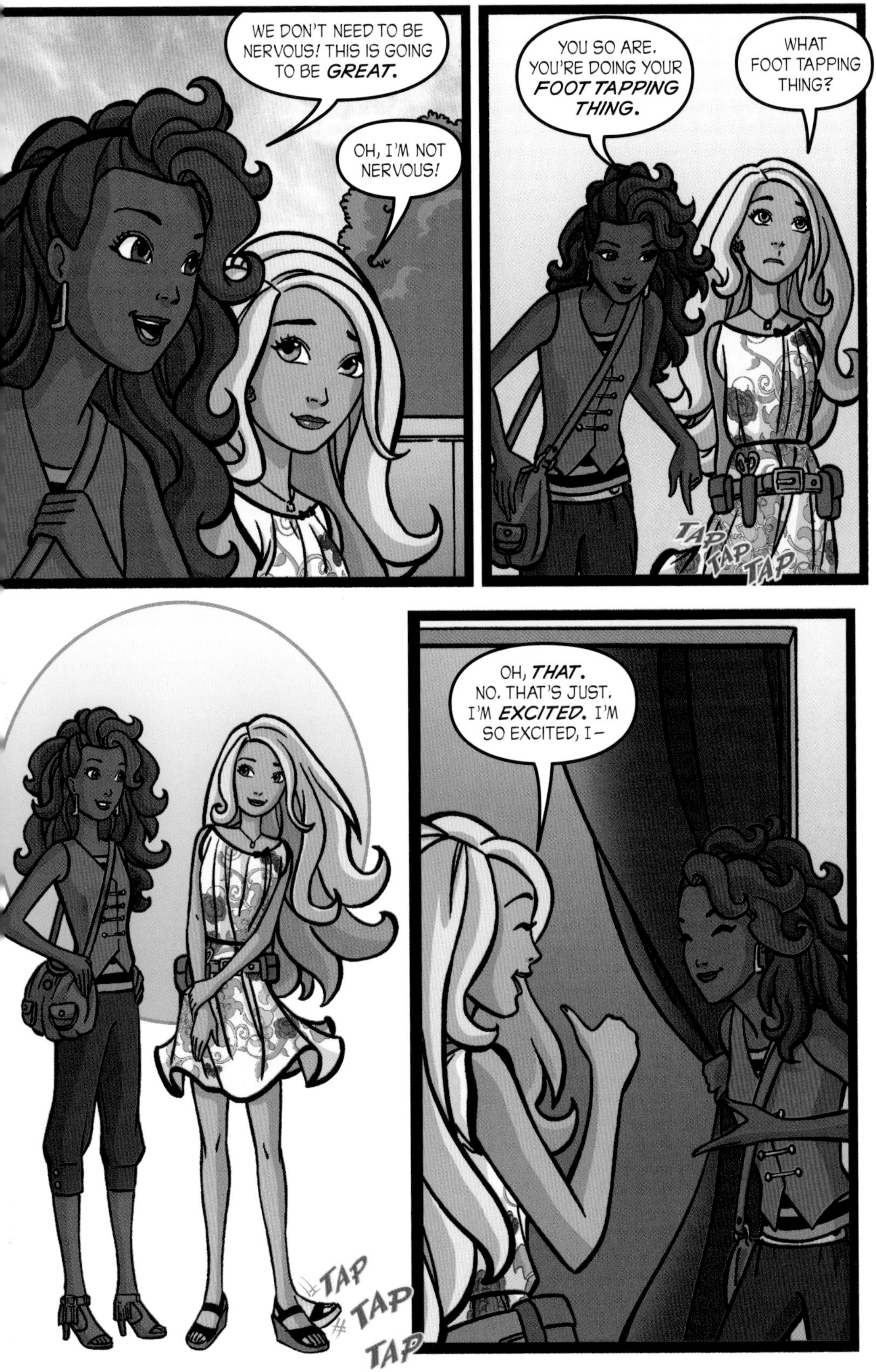
WE DON'T NEED TO BE NERVOUS! THIS IS GOING TO BE GREAT.
OH, I'M NOT NERVOUS!
YOU SO ARE. YOU'RE DOING YOUR FOOT TAPPING THING.
WHAT FOOT TAPPING THING?
TAP TAP TAP
TAP TAP TAP
OH, THAT. NO. THAT'S JUST. I'M EXCITED. I'M SO EXCITED, I—

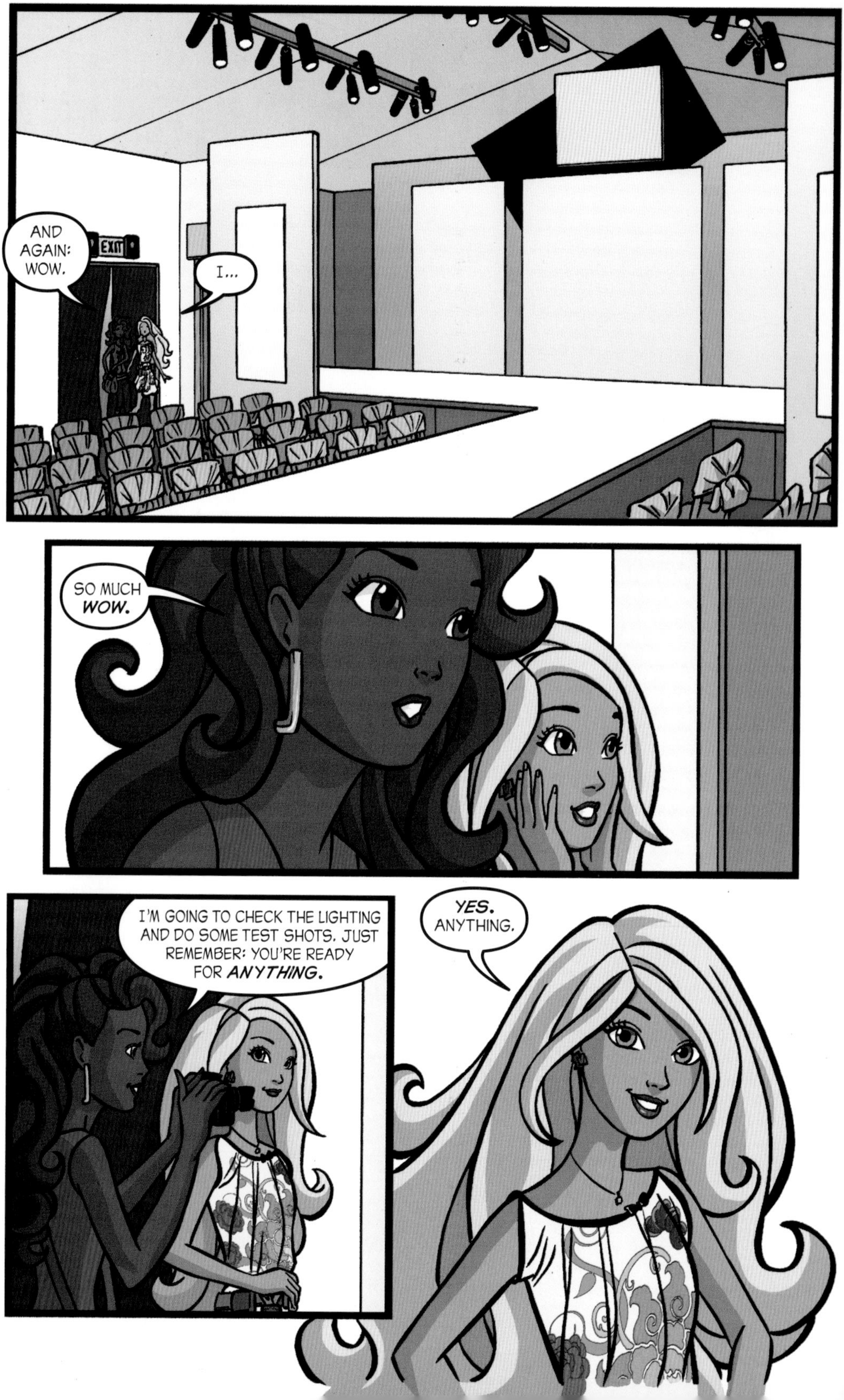
AND AGAIN: WOW.
I...
SO MUCH *WOW.*
I'M GOING TO CHECK THE LIGHTING AND DO SOME TEST SHOTS. JUST REMEMBER: YOU'RE READY FOR ***ANYTHING.***
YES. ANYTHING.
EXIT

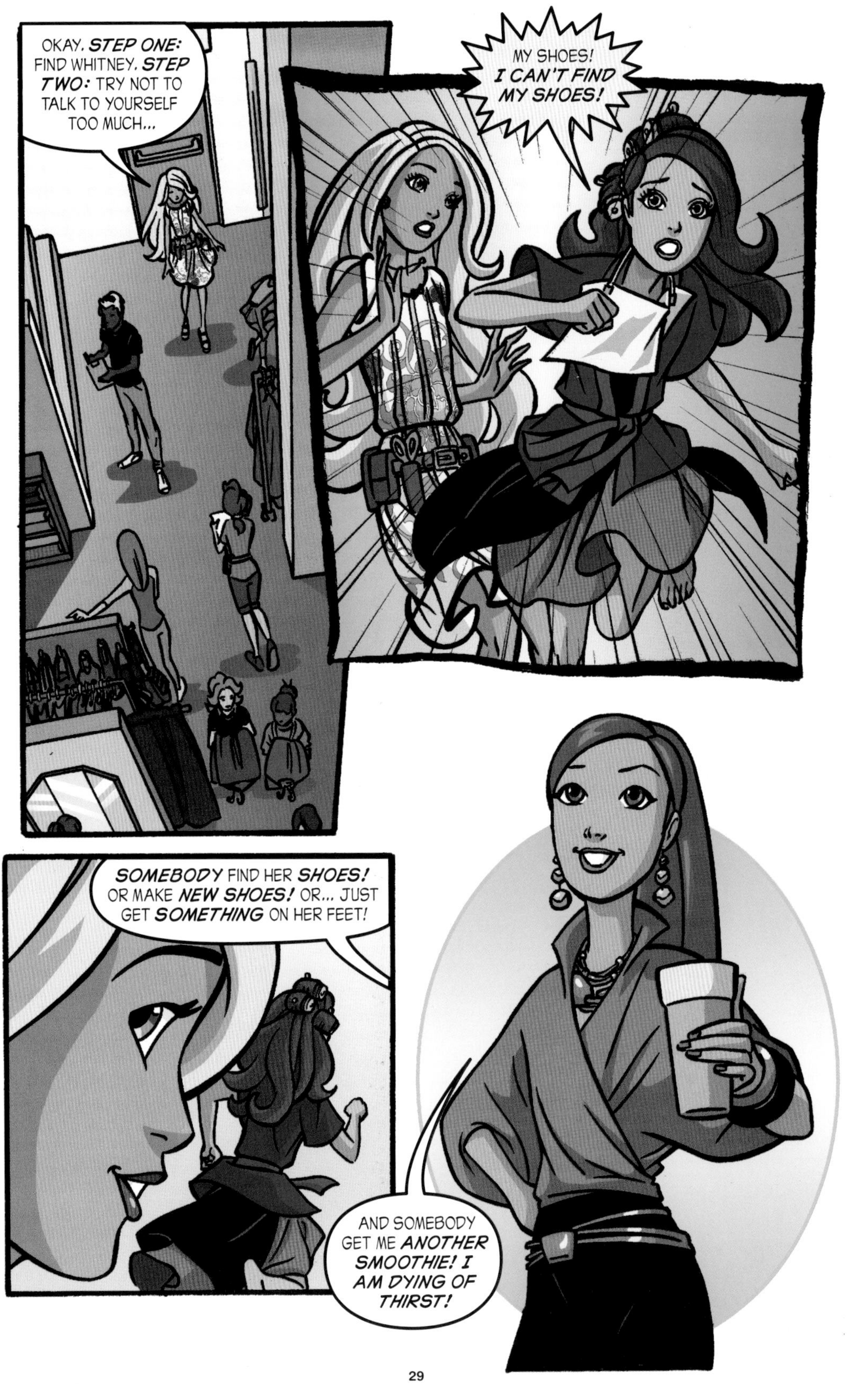
OKAY. STEP ONE: FIND WHITNEY. STEP TWO: TRY NOT TO TALK TO YOURSELF TOO MUCH...
MY SHOES! I CAN'T FIND MY SHOES!
SOMEBODY FIND HER SHOES! OR MAKE NEW SHOES! OR... JUST GET SOMETHING ON HER FEET!
AND SOMEBODY GET ME ANOTHER SMOOTHIE! I AM DYING OF THIRST!

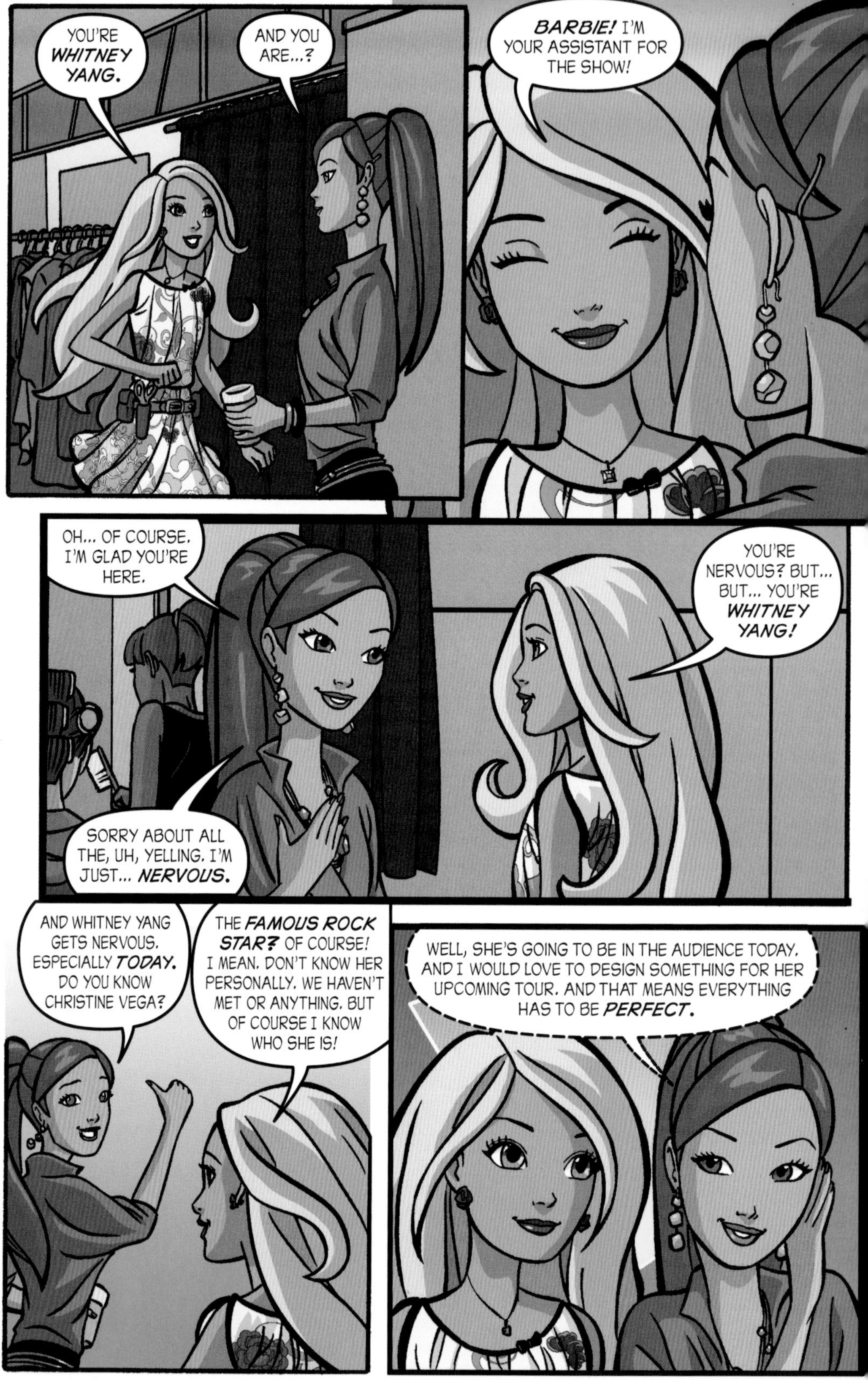
YOU'RE *WHITNEY YANG.*
AND YOU ARE...?
BARBIE! I'M YOUR ASSISTANT FOR THE SHOW!
OH... OF COURSE. I'M GLAD YOU'RE HERE.
SORRY ABOUT ALL THE, UH, YELLING. I'M JUST... *NERVOUS.*
YOU'RE NERVOUS? BUT... BUT... YOU'RE *WHITNEY YANG!*
AND WHITNEY YANG GETS NERVOUS. ESPECIALLY *TODAY.* DO YOU KNOW CHRISTINE VEGA?
THE *FAMOUS ROCK STAR?* OF COURSE! I MEAN, DON'T KNOW HER PERSONALLY. WE HAVEN'T MET OR ANYTHING. BUT OF COURSE I KNOW WHO SHE IS!
WELL, SHE'S GOING TO BE IN THE AUDIENCE TODAY, AND I WOULD LOVE TO DESIGN SOMETHING FOR HER UPCOMING TOUR. AND THAT MEANS EVERYTHING HAS TO BE *PERFECT.*

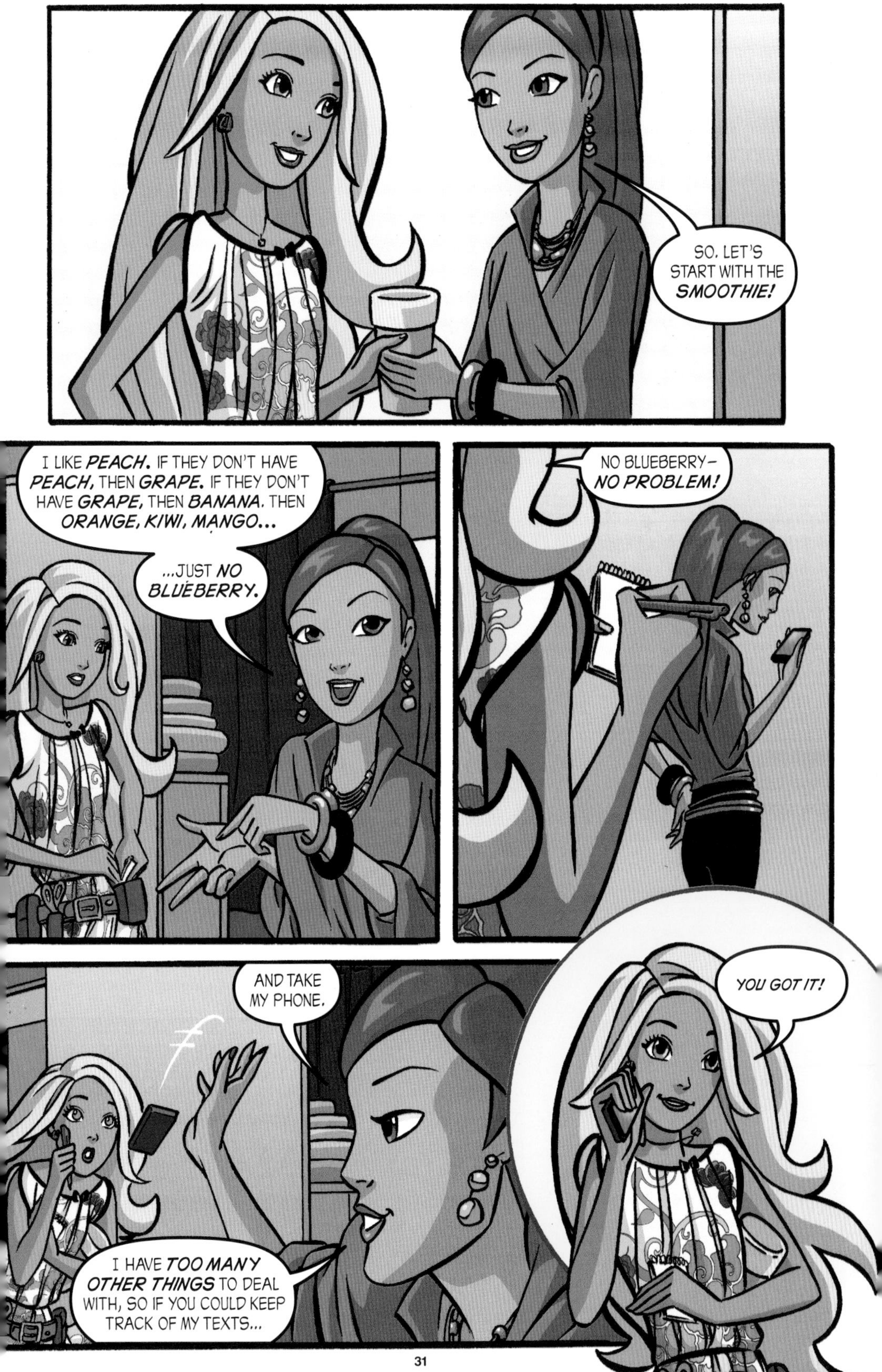
SO. LET'S START WITH THE SMOOTHIE!
I LIKE PEACH. IF THEY DON'T HAVE PEACH, THEN GRAPE. IF THEY DON'T HAVE GRAPE, THEN BANANA. THEN ORANGE, KIWI, MANGO...
...JUST NO BLUEBERRY.
NO BLUEBERRY– NO PROBLEM!
AND TAKE MY PHONE.
I HAVE TOO MANY OTHER THINGS TO DEAL WITH, SO IF YOU COULD KEEP TRACK OF MY TEXTS...
YOU GOT IT!

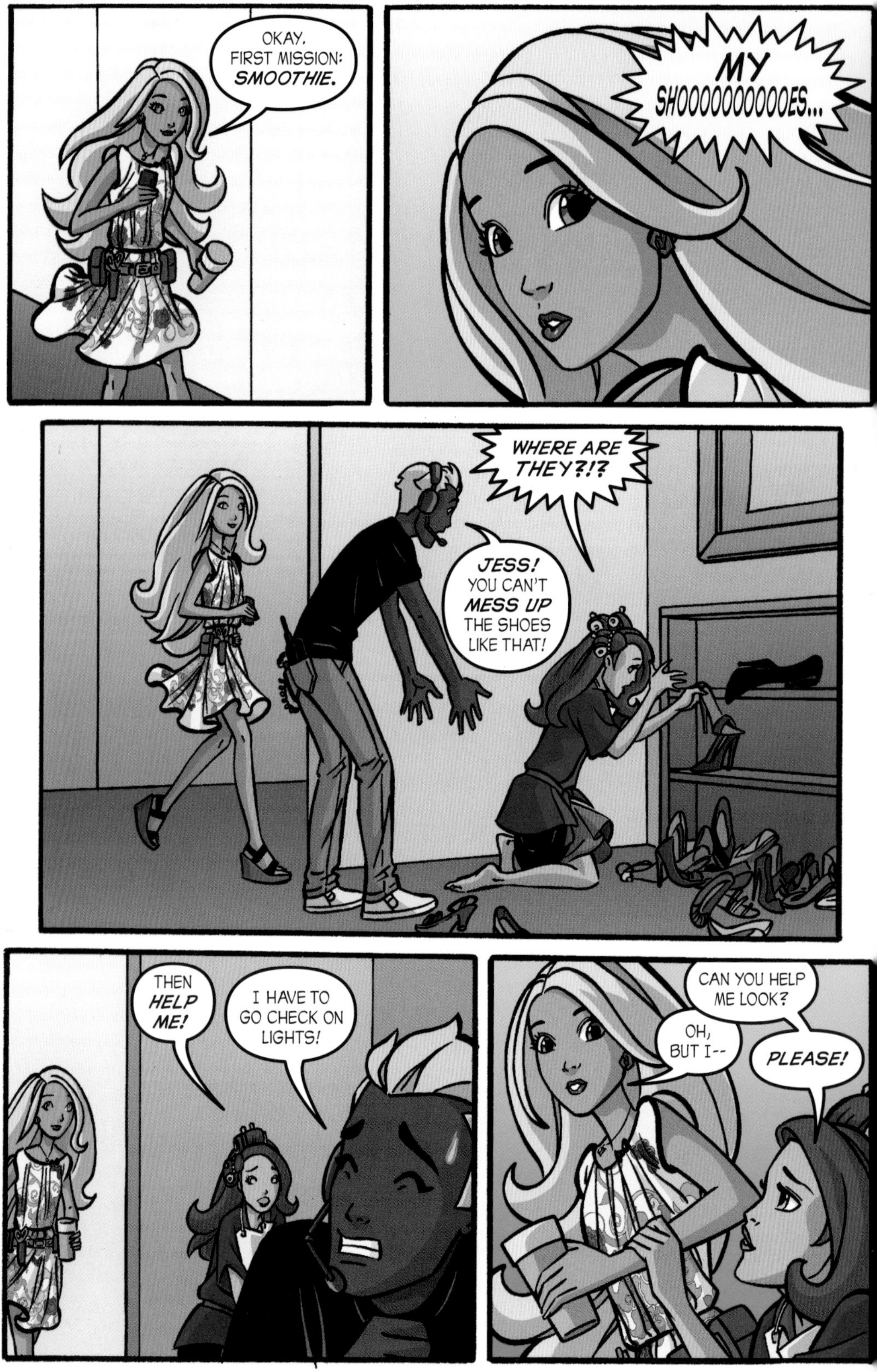
OKAY. FIRST MISSION: SMOOTHIE.
MY SHOOOOOOOOOOES...
WHERE ARE THEY?!?
JESS! YOU CAN'T MESS UP THE SHOES LIKE THAT!
THEN HELP ME!
I HAVE TO GO CHECK ON LIGHTS!
CAN YOU HELP ME LOOK?
OH, BUT I--
PLEASE!

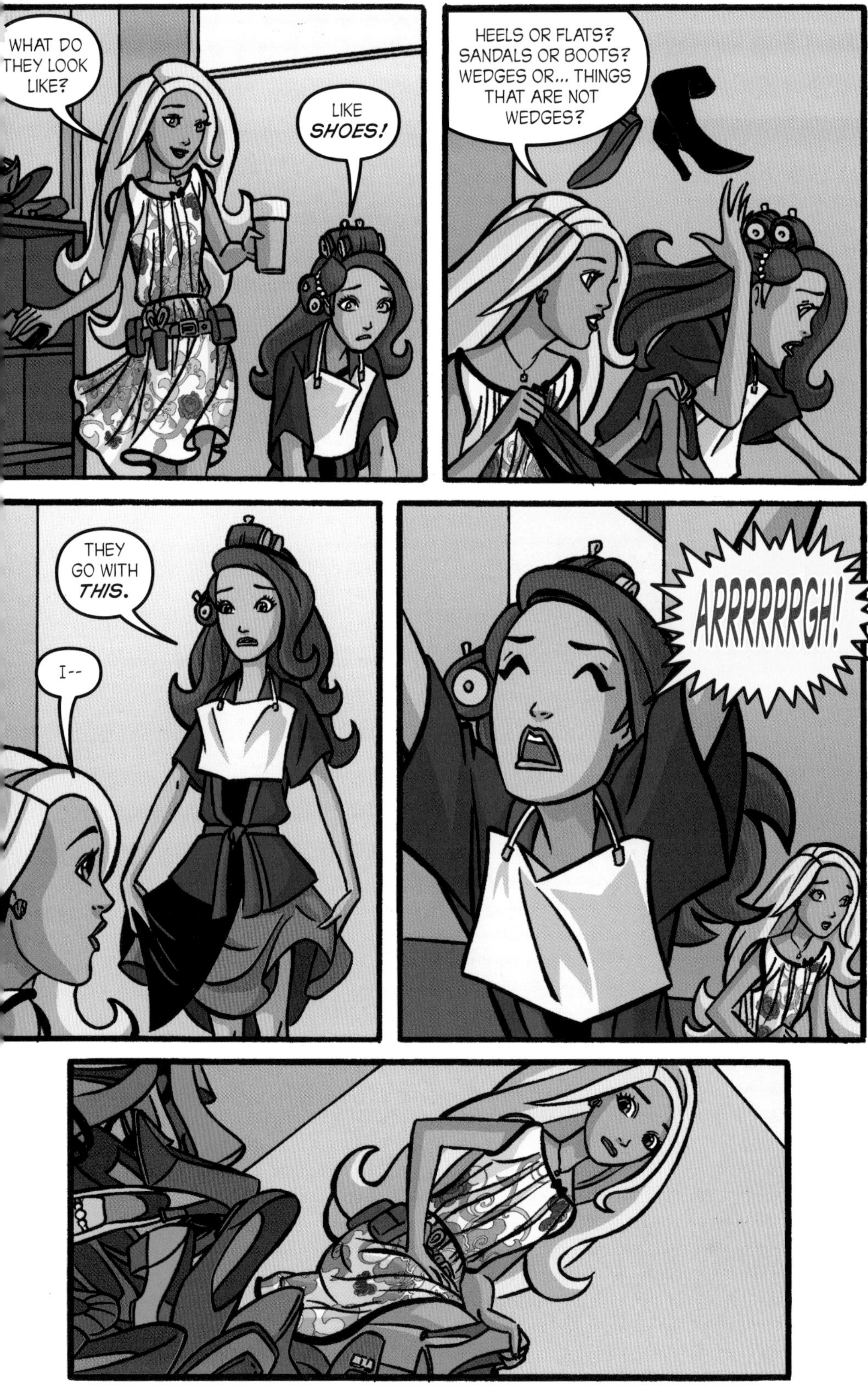
WHAT DO THEY LOOK LIKE?
LIKE *SHOES!*
HEELS OR FLATS? SANDALS OR BOOTS? WEDGES OR... THINGS THAT ARE NOT WEDGES?
THEY GO WITH *THIS.*
I--
ARRRRRRGH!

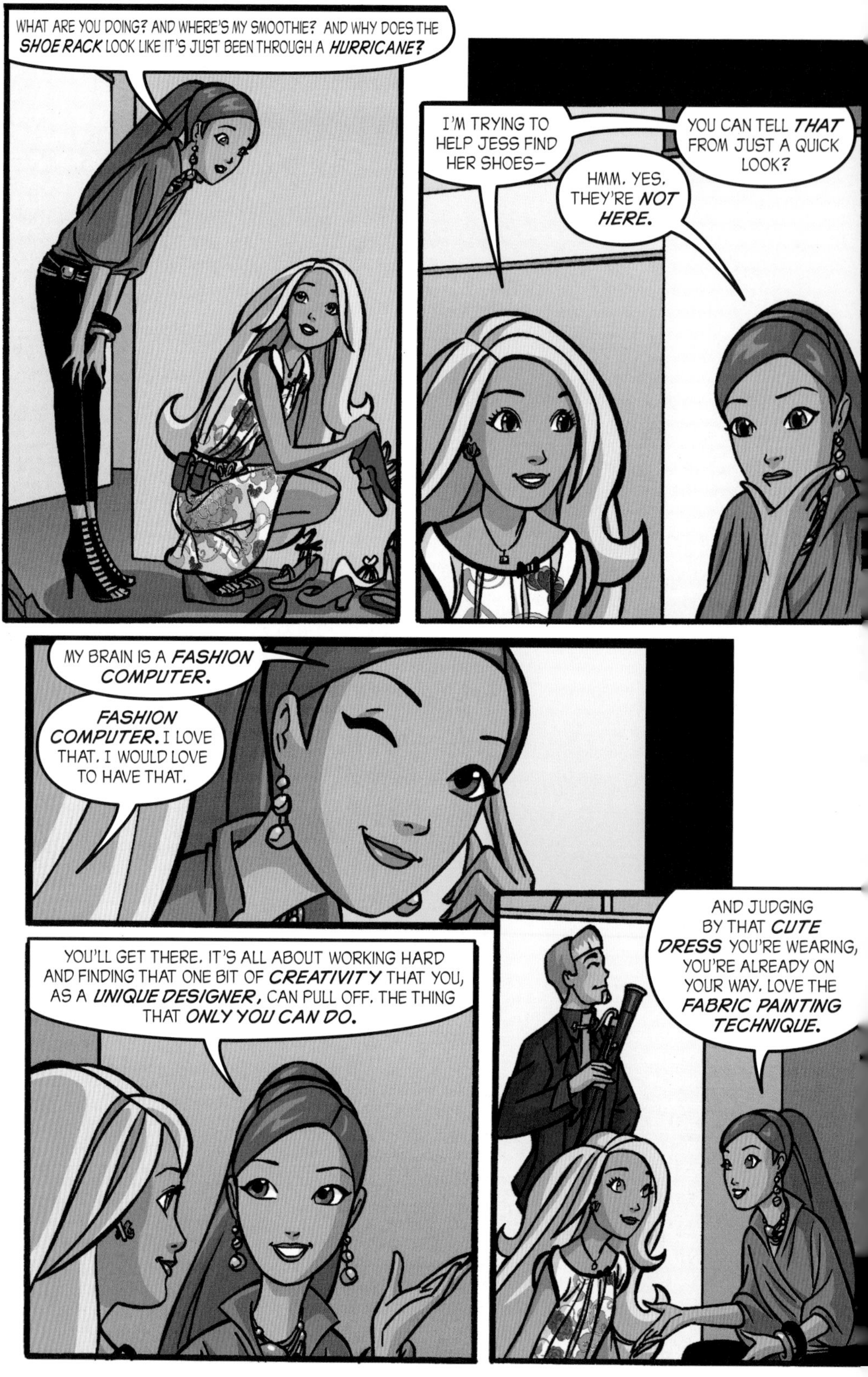
WHAT ARE YOU DOING? AND WHERE'S MY SMOOTHIE? AND WHY DOES THE SHOE RACK LOOK LIKE IT'S JUST BEEN THROUGH A HURRICANE?
I'M TRYING TO HELP JESS FIND HER SHOES–
HMM. YES. THEY'RE NOT HERE.
YOU CAN TELL THAT FROM JUST A QUICK LOOK?
MY BRAIN IS A FASHION COMPUTER.
FASHION COMPUTER. I LOVE THAT. I WOULD LOVE TO HAVE THAT.
YOU'LL GET THERE. IT'S ALL ABOUT WORKING HARD AND FINDING THAT ONE BIT OF CREATIVITY THAT YOU, AS A UNIQUE DESIGNER, CAN PULL OFF. THE THING THAT ONLY YOU CAN DO.
AND JUDGING BY THAT CUTE DRESS YOU'RE WEARING, YOU'RE ALREADY ON YOUR WAY. LOVE THE FABRIC PAINTING TECHNIQUE.

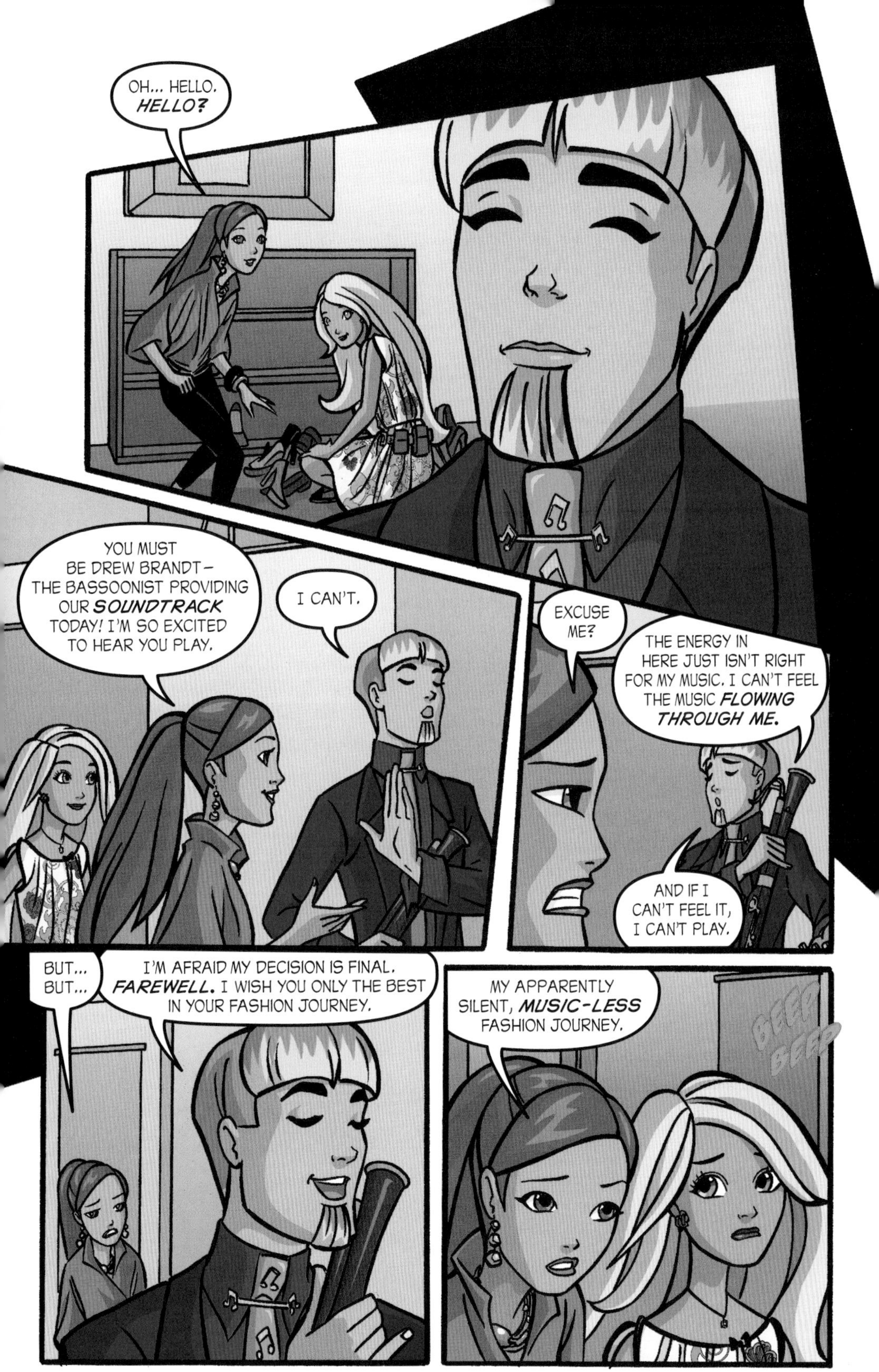
OH... HELLO. HELLO?
YOU MUST BE DREW BRANDT— THE BASSOONIST PROVIDING OUR SOUNDTRACK TODAY! I'M SO EXCITED TO HEAR YOU PLAY.
I CAN'T.
EXCUSE ME?
THE ENERGY IN HERE JUST ISN'T RIGHT FOR MY MUSIC. I CAN'T FEEL THE MUSIC FLOWING THROUGH ME.
AND IF I CAN'T FEEL IT, I CAN'T PLAY.
BUT... BUT...
I'M AFRAID MY DECISION IS FINAL. FAREWELL. I WISH YOU ONLY THE BEST IN YOUR FASHION JOURNEY.
MY APPARENTLY SILENT, MUSIC-LESS FASHION JOURNEY.
BEEP BEEP

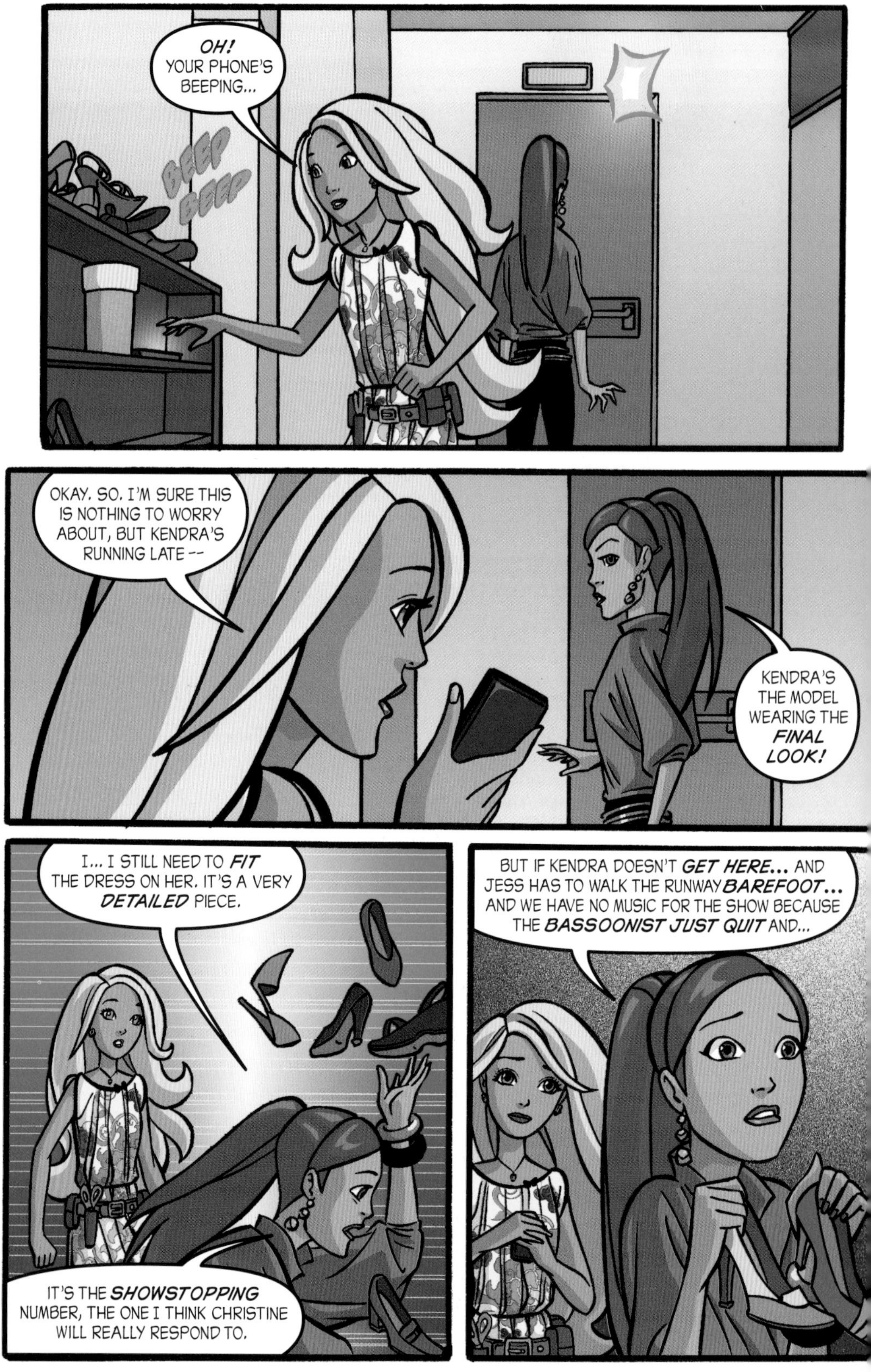
OH! YOUR PHONE'S BEEPING...
BEEP BEEP
OKAY. SO. I'M SURE THIS IS NOTHING TO WORRY ABOUT, BUT KENDRA'S RUNNING LATE --
KENDRA'S THE MODEL WEARING THE FINAL LOOK!
I... I STILL NEED TO FIT THE DRESS ON HER. IT'S A VERY DETAILED PIECE.
IT'S THE SHOWSTOPPING NUMBER, THE ONE I THINK CHRISTINE WILL REALLY RESPOND TO.
BUT IF KENDRA DOESN'T GET HERE... AND JESS HAS TO WALK THE RUNWAY BAREFOOT... AND WE HAVE NO MUSIC FOR THE SHOW BECAUSE THE BASSOONIST JUST QUIT AND...

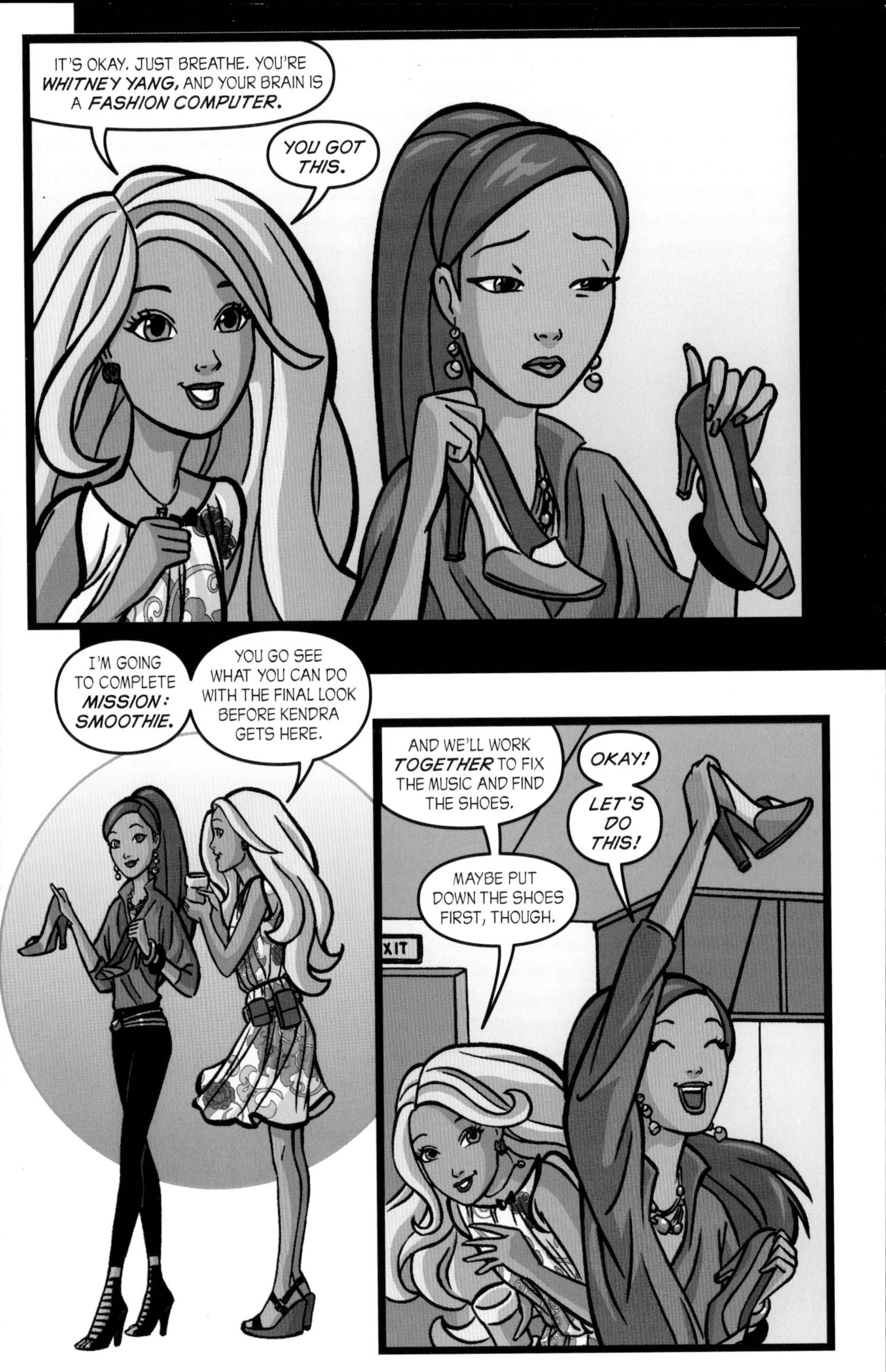
IT'S OKAY. JUST BREATHE. YOU'RE WHITNEY YANG, AND YOUR BRAIN IS A FASHION COMPUTER.
YOU GOT THIS.
I'M GOING TO COMPLETE MISSION: SMOOTHIE.
YOU GO SEE WHAT YOU CAN DO WITH THE FINAL LOOK BEFORE KENDRA GETS HERE.
AND WE'LL WORK TOGETHER TO FIX THE MUSIC AND FIND THE SHOES.
OKAY!
LET'S DO THIS!
MAYBE PUT DOWN THE SHOES FIRST, THOUGH.
EXIT

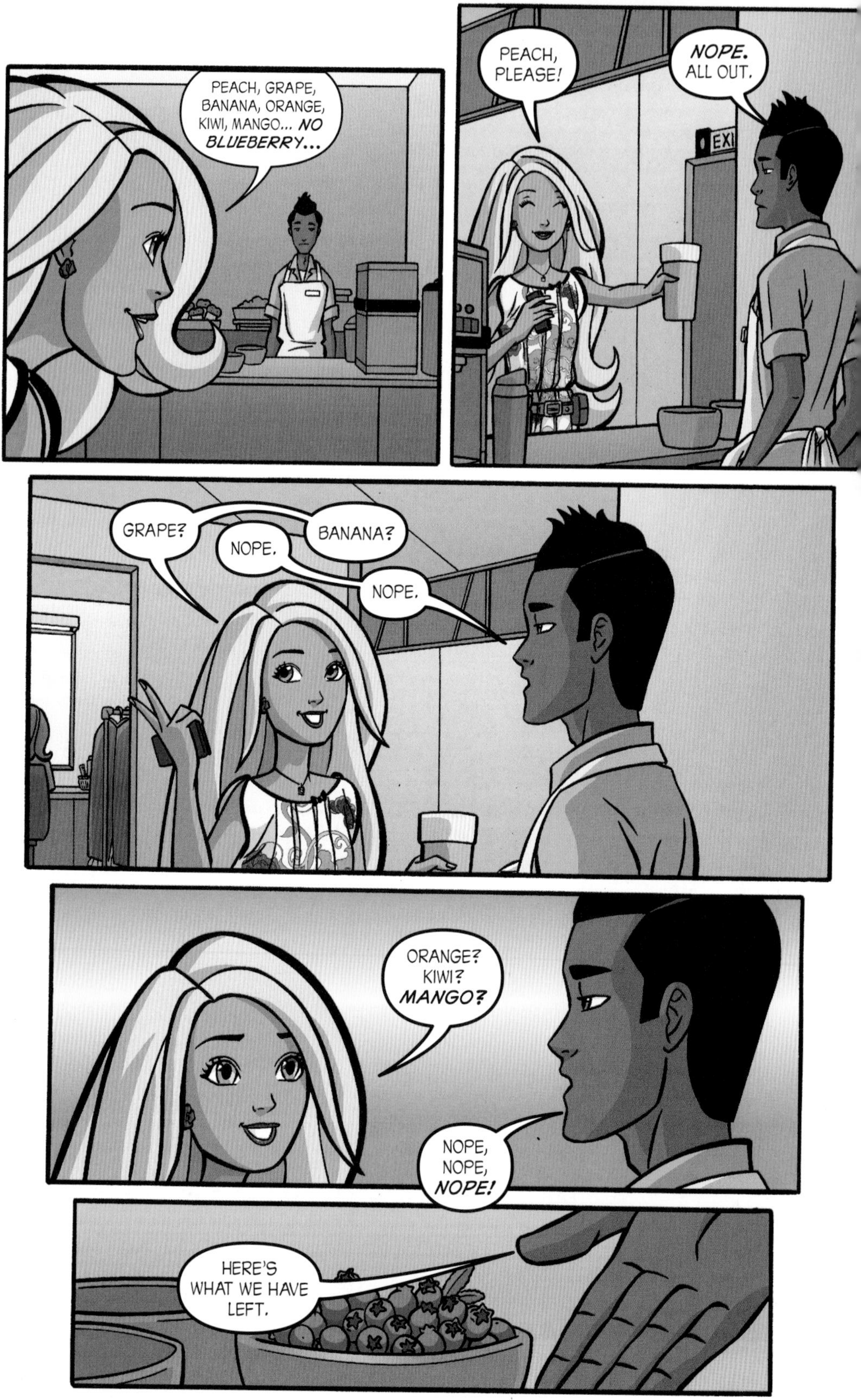
PEACH, GRAPE, BANANA, ORANGE, KIWI, MANGO... NO BLUEBERRY...
PEACH, PLEASE!
NOPE. ALL OUT.
EXI
GRAPE?
NOPE.
BANANA?
NOPE.
ORANGE? KIWI? MANGO?
NOPE, NOPE, NOPE!
HERE'S WHAT WE HAVE LEFT.

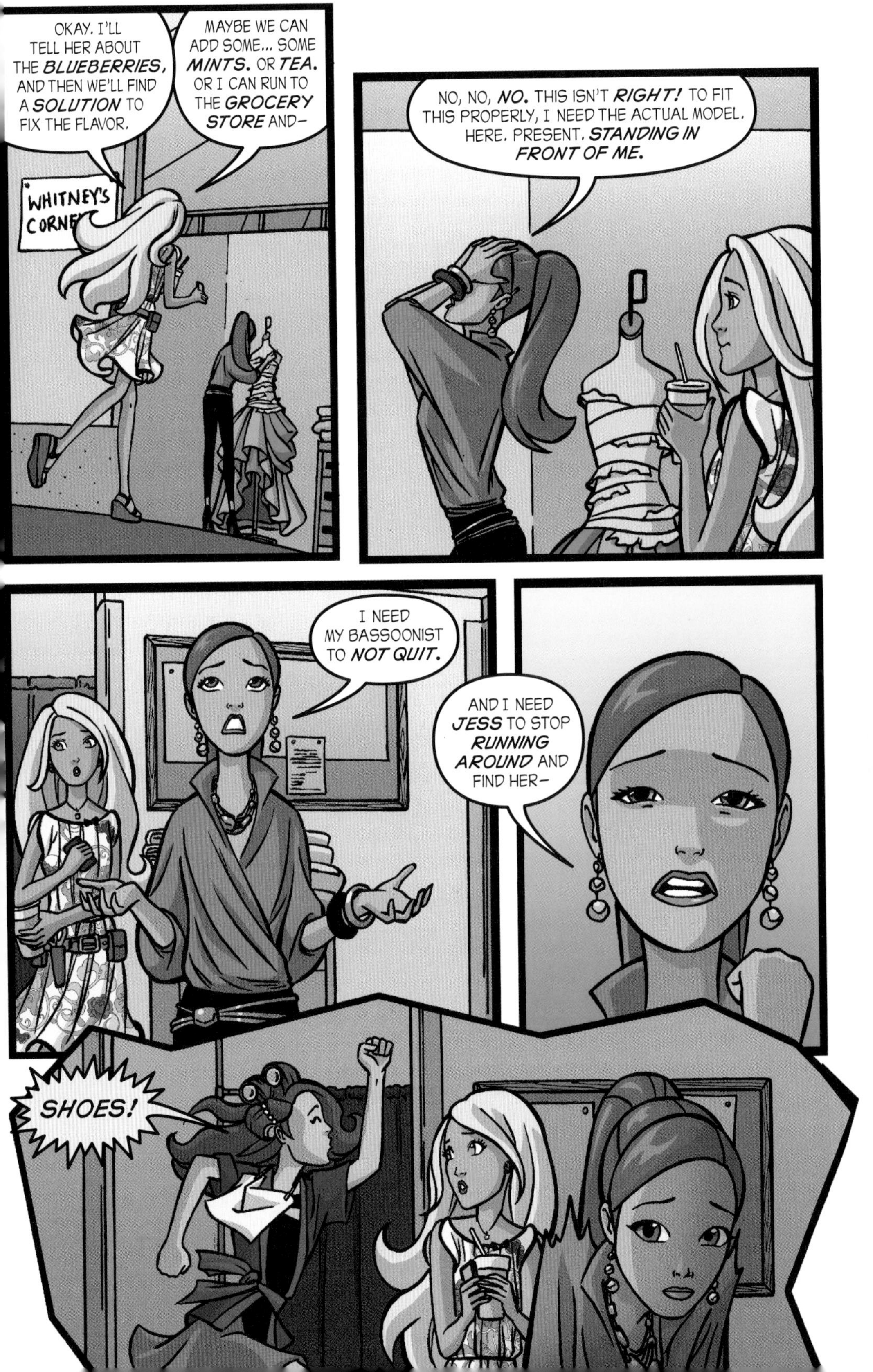
OKAY. I'LL TELL HER ABOUT THE BLUEBERRIES, AND THEN WE'LL FIND A SOLUTION TO FIX THE FLAVOR.
MAYBE WE CAN ADD SOME... SOME MINTS. OR TEA. OR I CAN RUN TO THE GROCERY STORE AND–
WHITNEY'S CORNE
NO, NO, NO. THIS ISN'T RIGHT! TO FIT THIS PROPERLY, I NEED THE ACTUAL MODEL. HERE. PRESENT. STANDING IN FRONT OF ME.
I NEED MY BASSOONIST TO NOT QUIT.
AND I NEED JESS TO STOP RUNNING AROUND AND FIND HER–
SHOES!

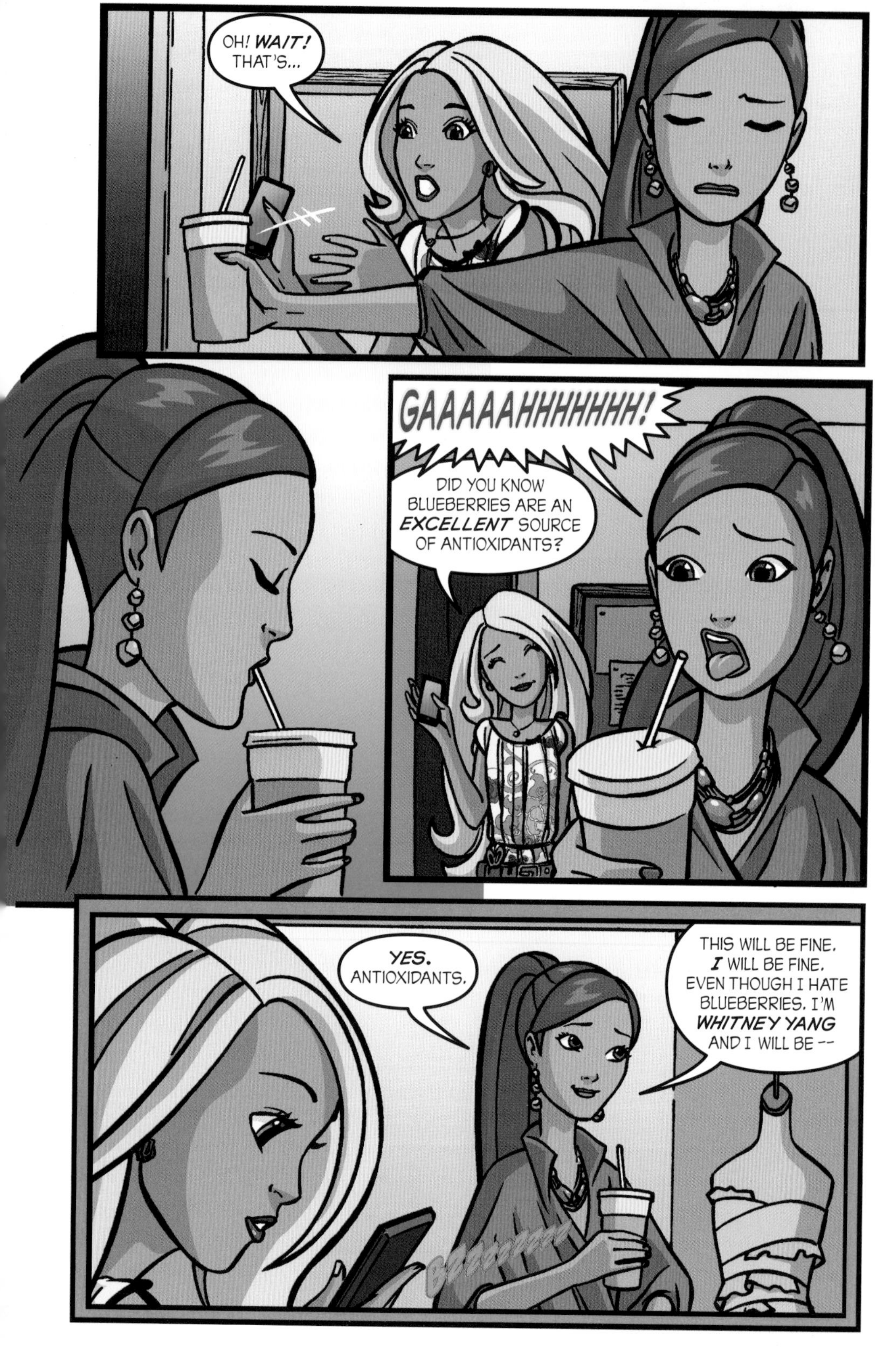
OH! WAIT! THAT'S...
GAAAAAHHHHHHH!
DID YOU KNOW BLUEBERRIES ARE AN EXCELLENT SOURCE OF ANTIOXIDANTS?
YES. ANTIOXIDANTS.
THIS WILL BE FINE. I WILL BE FINE. EVEN THOUGH I HATE BLUEBERRIES. I'M WHITNEY YANG AND I WILL BE --

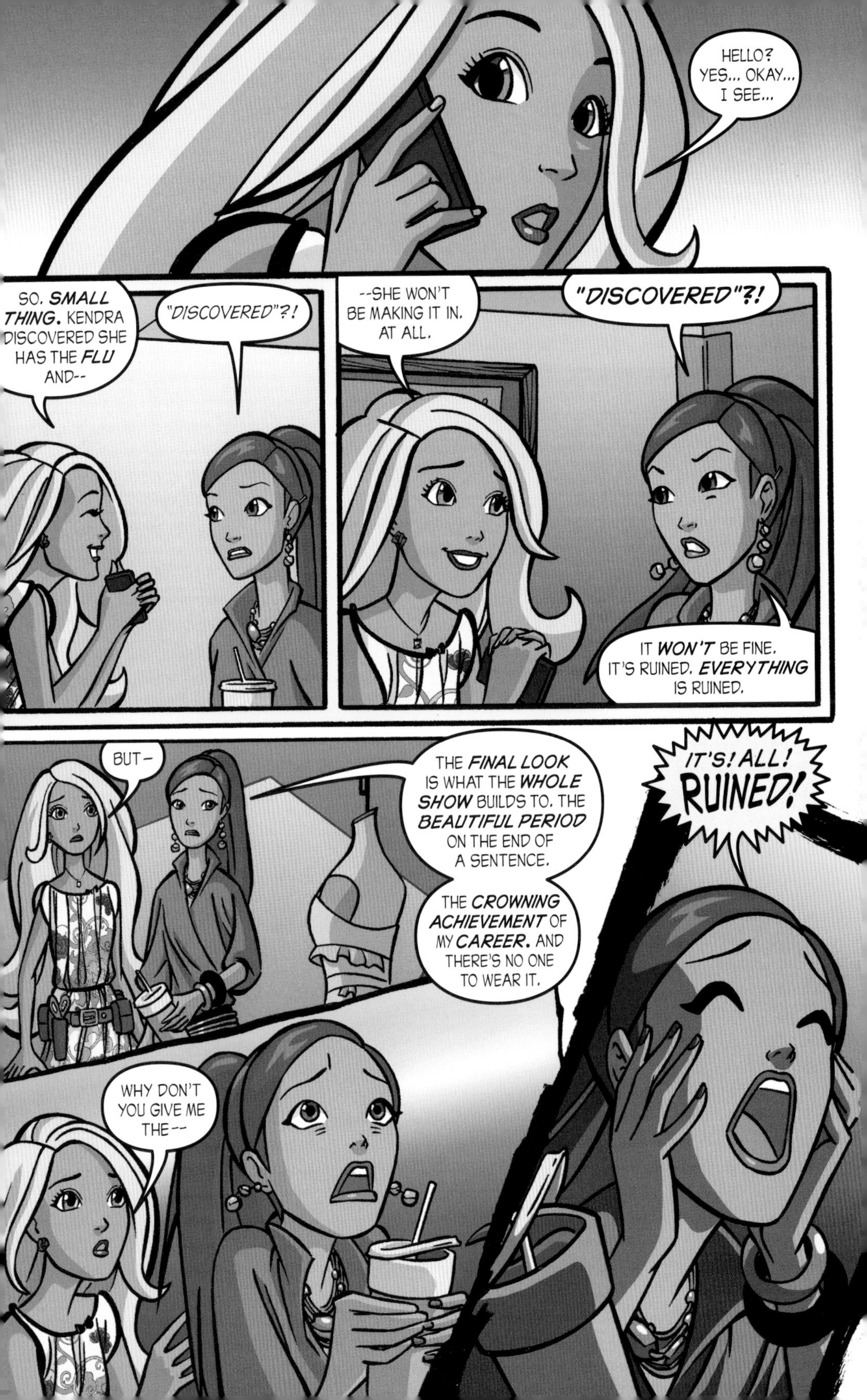
HELLO? YES... OKAY... I SEE...
SO. SMALL THING. KENDRA DISCOVERED SHE HAS THE FLU AND--
"DISCOVERED"?!
--SHE WON'T BE MAKING IT IN. AT ALL.
"DISCOVERED"?!
IT WON'T BE FINE. IT'S RUINED. EVERYTHING IS RUINED.
BUT—
THE FINAL LOOK IS WHAT THE WHOLE SHOW BUILDS TO. THE BEAUTIFUL PERIOD ON THE END OF A SENTENCE.
THE CROWNING ACHIEVEMENT OF MY CAREER. AND THERE'S NO ONE TO WEAR IT.
IT'S! ALL! RUINED!
WHY DON'T YOU GIVE ME THE--

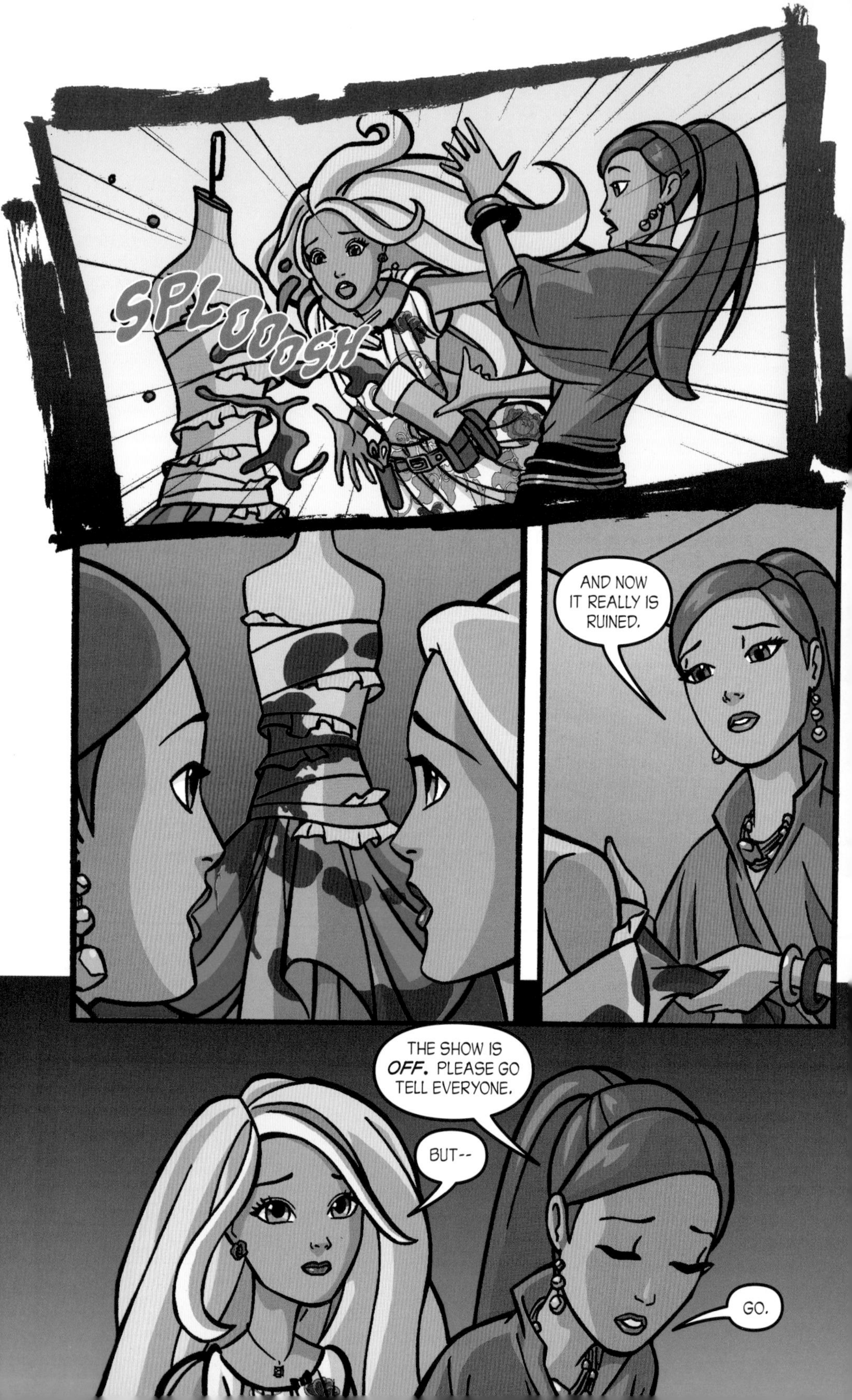
SPLOOOOSH
AND NOW IT REALLY IS RUINED.
THE SHOW IS OFF. PLEASE GO TELL EVERYONE.
BUT--
GO.

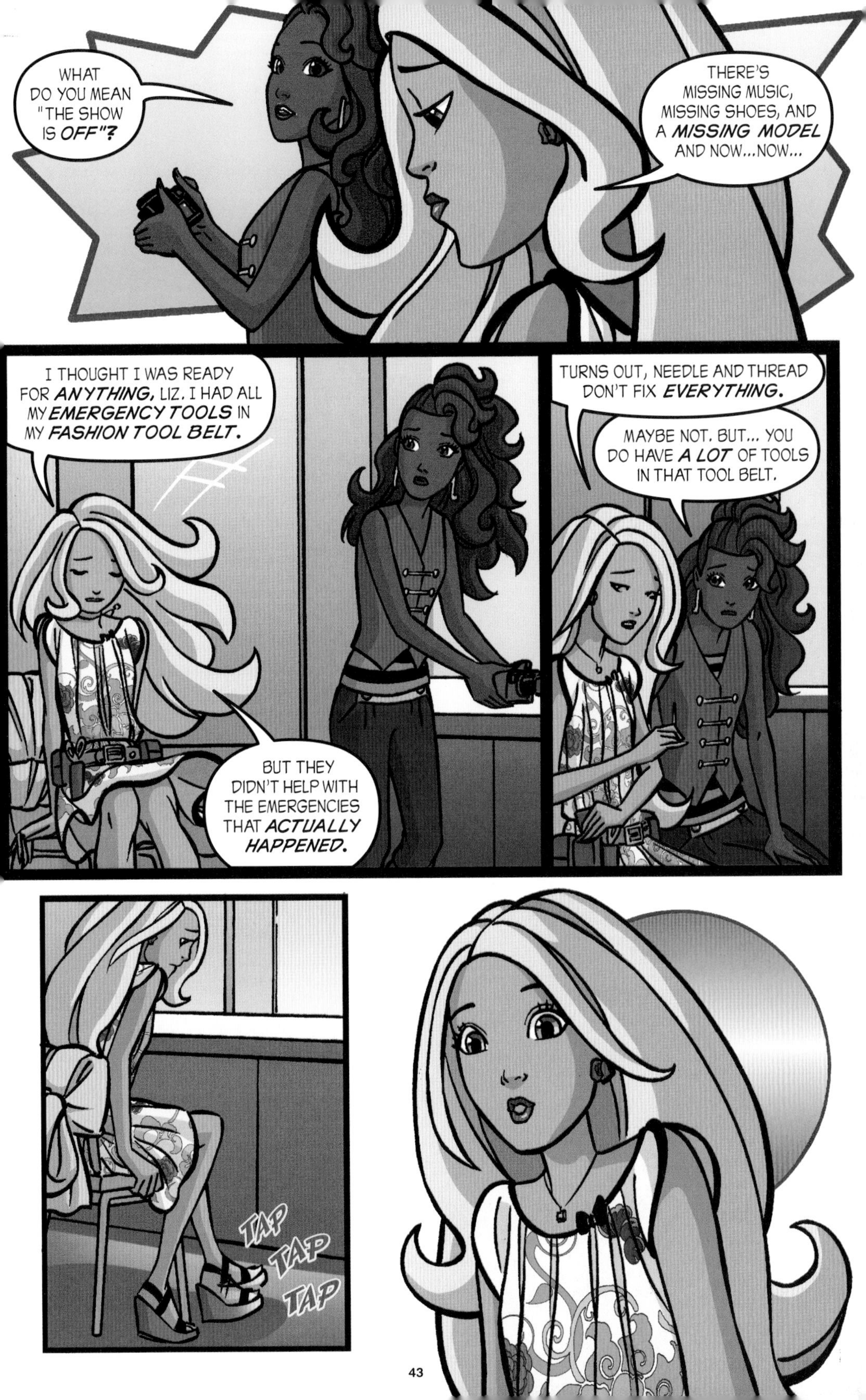
WHAT DO YOU MEAN "THE SHOW IS *OFF*"?
THERE'S MISSING MUSIC, MISSING SHOES, AND A *MISSING MODEL* AND NOW...NOW...
I THOUGHT I WAS READY FOR *ANYTHING,* LIZ. I HAD ALL MY *EMERGENCY TOOLS* IN MY *FASHION TOOL BELT*.
BUT THEY DIDN'T HELP WITH THE EMERGENCIES THAT *ACTUALLY HAPPENED*.
TURNS OUT, NEEDLE AND THREAD DON'T FIX *EVERYTHING*.
MAYBE NOT. BUT... YOU DO HAVE *A LOT* OF TOOLS IN THAT TOOL BELT.
TAP
TAP
TAP

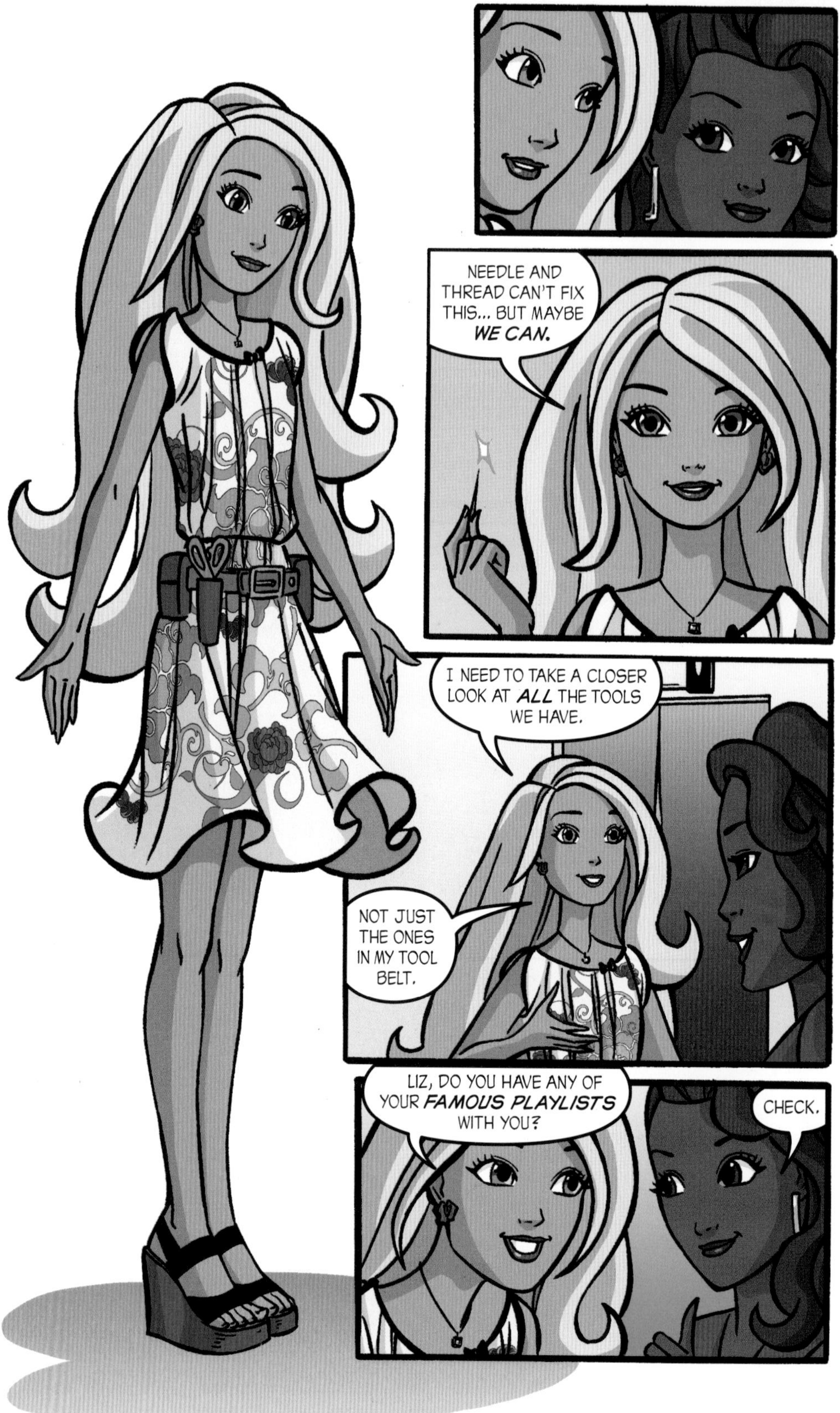
NEEDLE AND THREAD CAN'T FIX THIS... BUT MAYBE **WE CAN.**
I NEED TO TAKE A CLOSER LOOK AT ***ALL*** THE TOOLS WE HAVE.
NOT JUST THE ONES IN MY TOOL BELT.
LIZ, DO YOU HAVE ANY OF YOUR ***FAMOUS PLAYLISTS*** WITH YOU?
CHECK.

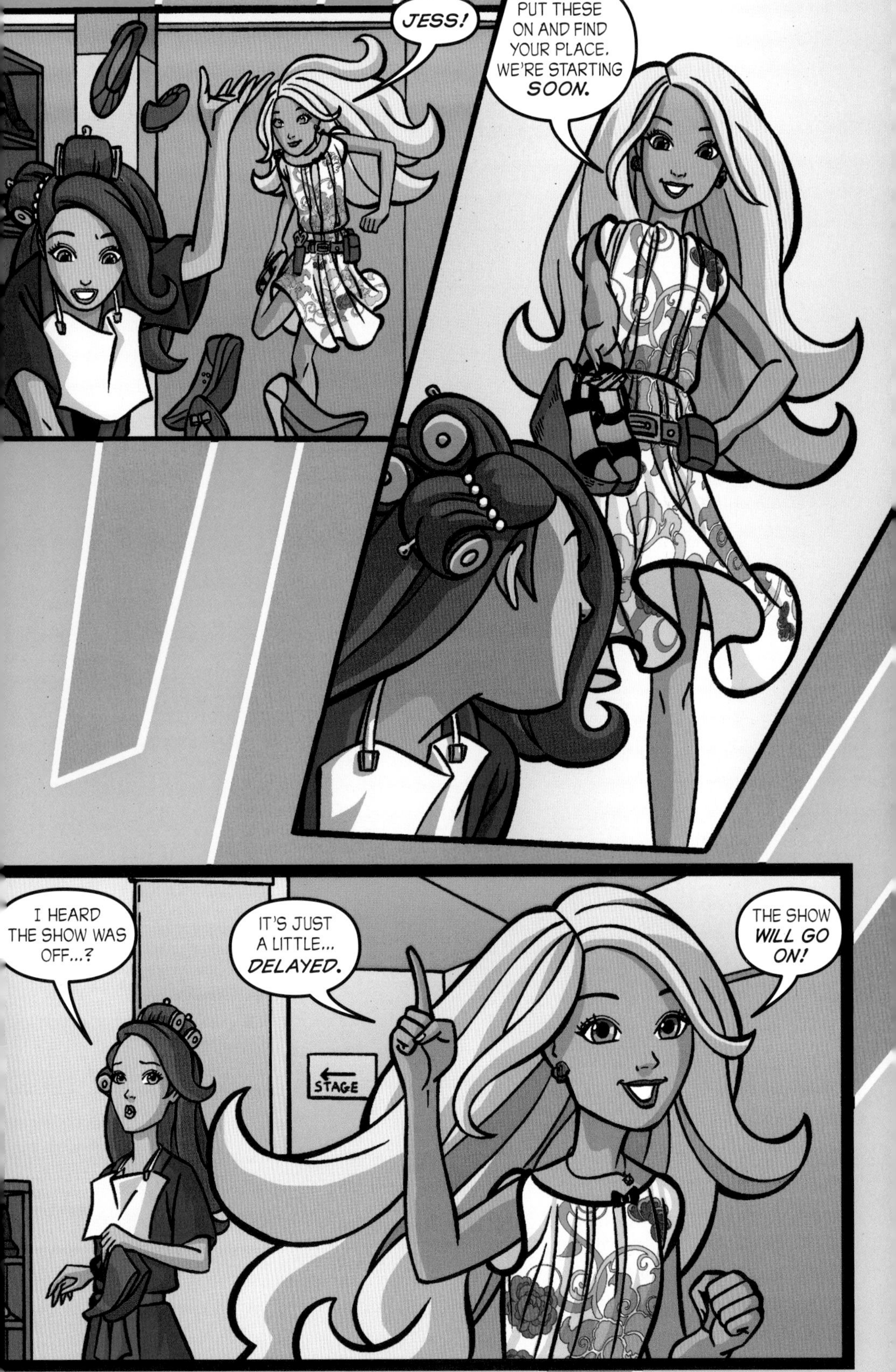
JESS!
PUT THESE ON AND FIND YOUR PLACE. WE'RE STARTING SOON.
I HEARD THE SHOW WAS OFF...?
IT'S JUST A LITTLE... DELAYED.
THE SHOW WILL GO ON!
STAGE

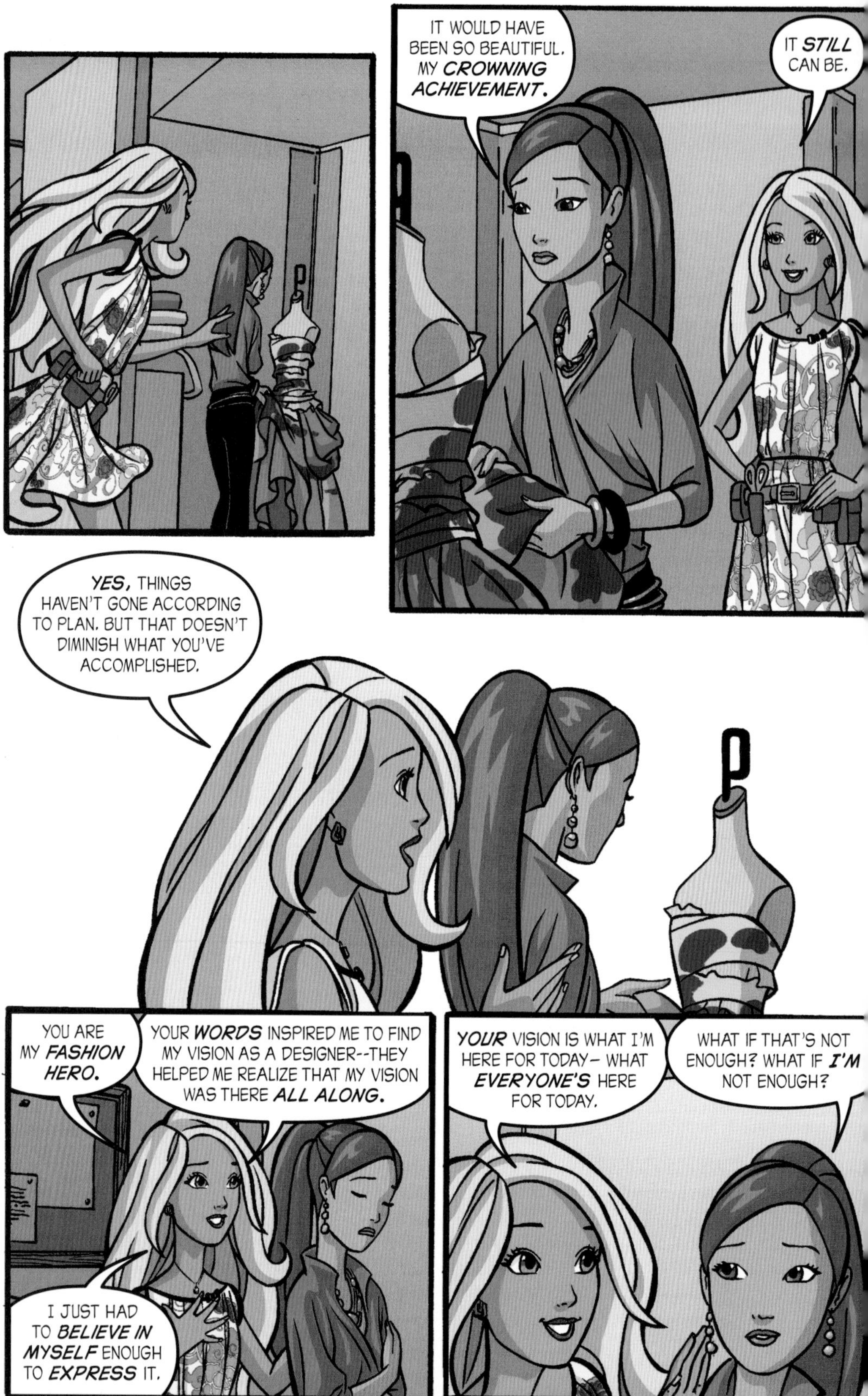
IT WOULD HAVE BEEN SO BEAUTIFUL. MY *CROWNING ACHIEVEMENT*.
IT *STILL* CAN BE.
YES, THINGS HAVEN'T GONE ACCORDING TO PLAN. BUT THAT DOESN'T DIMINISH WHAT YOU'VE ACCOMPLISHED.
YOU ARE MY *FASHION HERO.*
YOUR *WORDS* INSPIRED ME TO FIND MY VISION AS A DESIGNER--THEY HELPED ME REALIZE THAT MY VISION WAS THERE *ALL ALONG.*
I JUST HAD TO *BELIEVE IN MYSELF* ENOUGH TO *EXPRESS* IT.
YOUR VISION IS WHAT I'M HERE FOR TODAY– WHAT *EVERYONE'S* HERE FOR TODAY.
WHAT IF THAT'S NOT ENOUGH? WHAT IF *I'M* NOT ENOUGH?

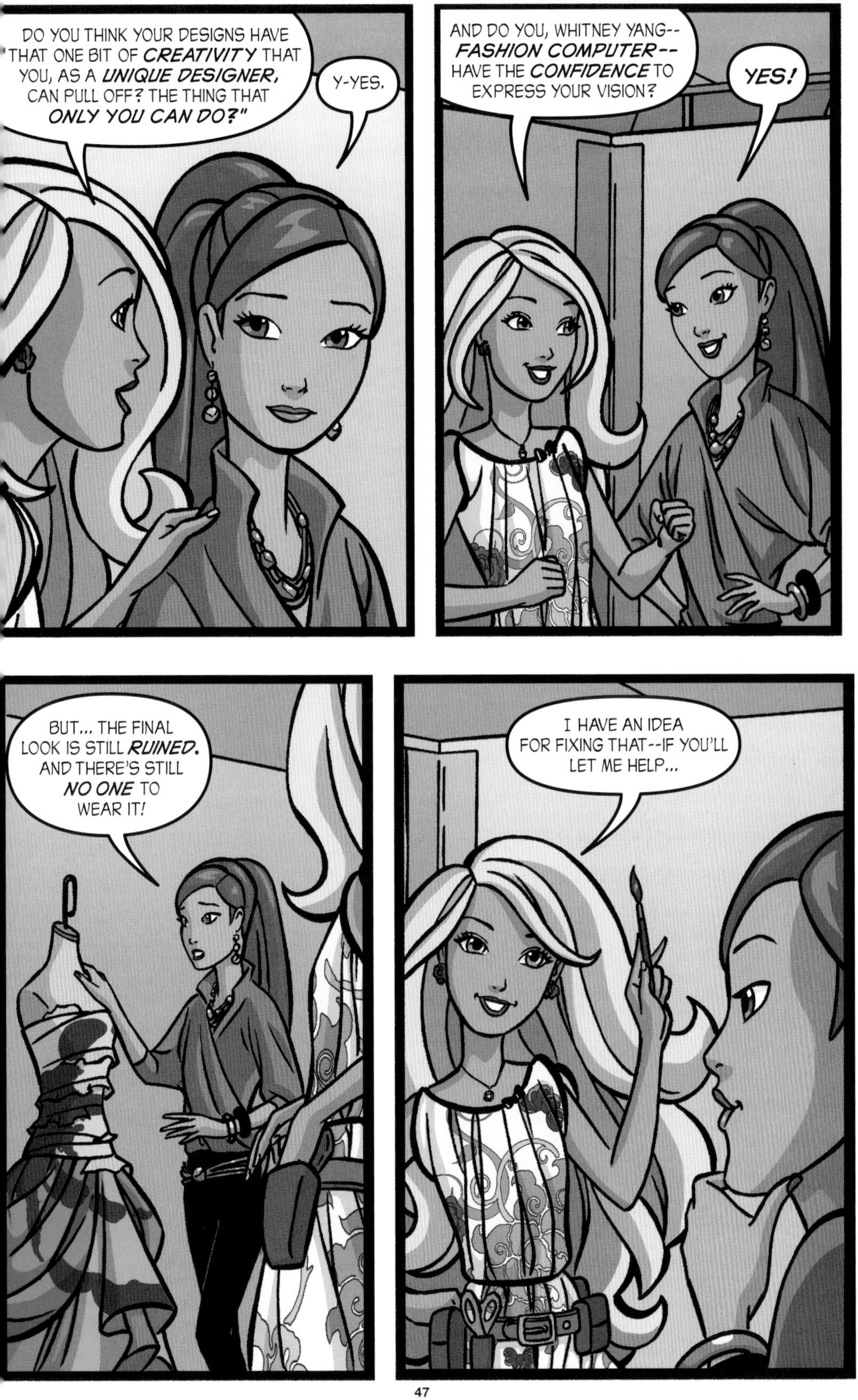
DO YOU THINK YOUR DESIGNS HAVE THAT ONE BIT OF CREATIVITY THAT YOU, AS A UNIQUE DESIGNER, CAN PULL OFF? THE THING THAT ONLY YOU CAN DO?"
Y-YES.
AND DO YOU, WHITNEY YANG-- FASHION COMPUTER-- HAVE THE CONFIDENCE TO EXPRESS YOUR VISION?
YES!
BUT... THE FINAL LOOK IS STILL RUINED. AND THERE'S STILL NO ONE TO WEAR IT!
I HAVE AN IDEA FOR FIXING THAT--IF YOU'LL LET ME HELP...

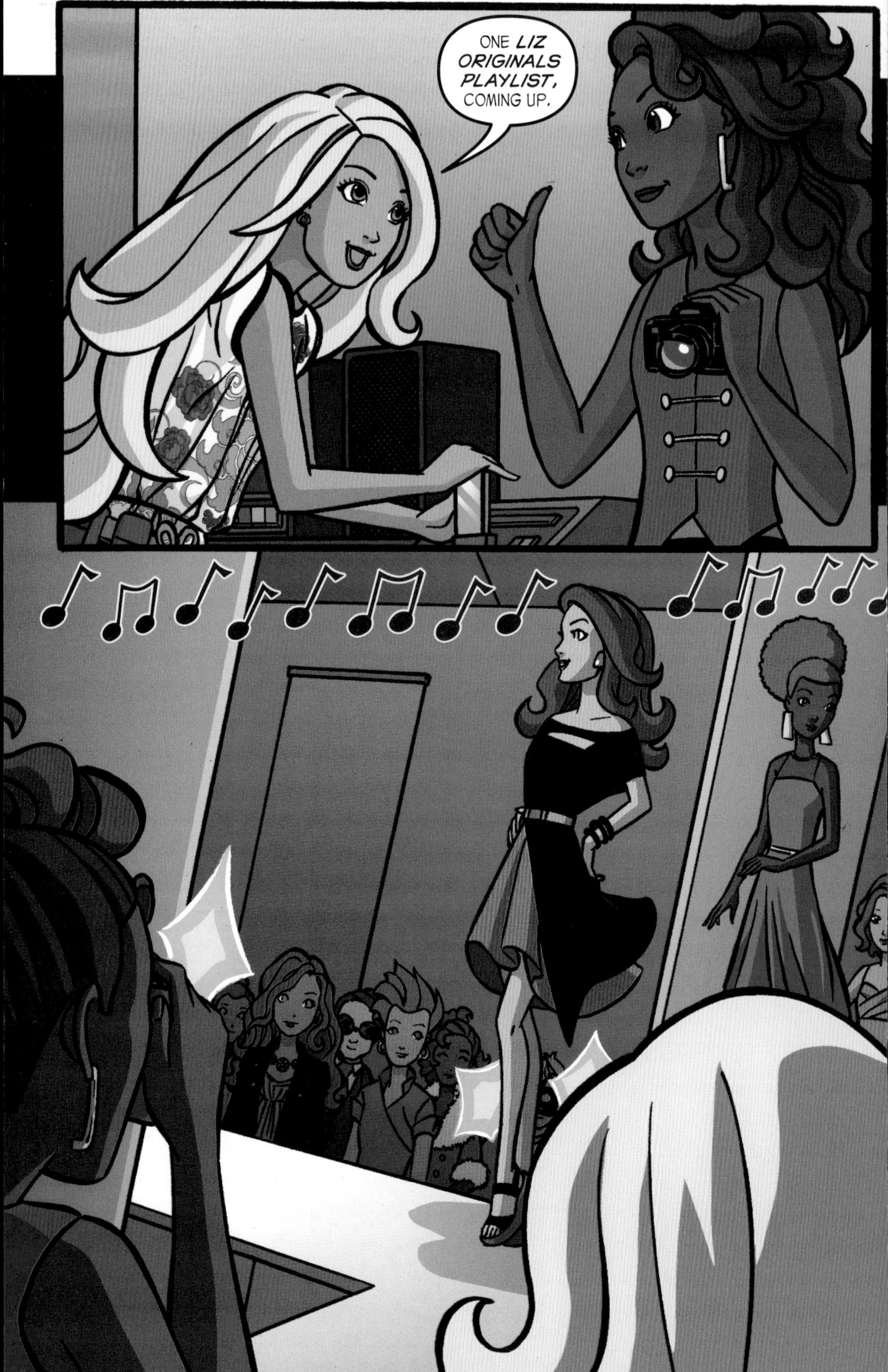
ONE LIZ ORIGINALS PLAYLIST, COMING UP.

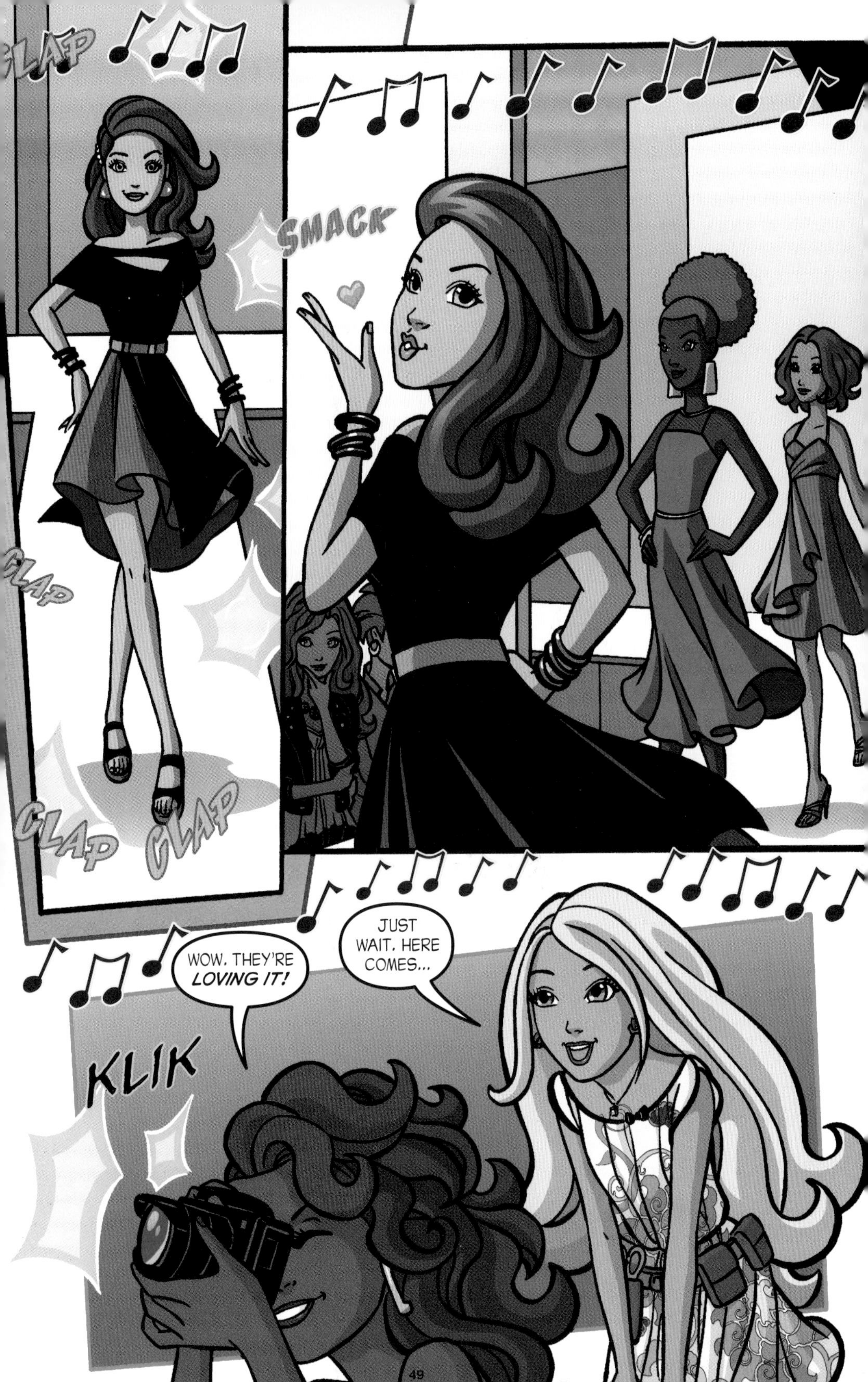
CLAP
SMACK
CLAP
CLAP
CLAP
WOW. THEY'RE *LOVING IT!*
JUST WAIT. HERE COMES...
KLIK

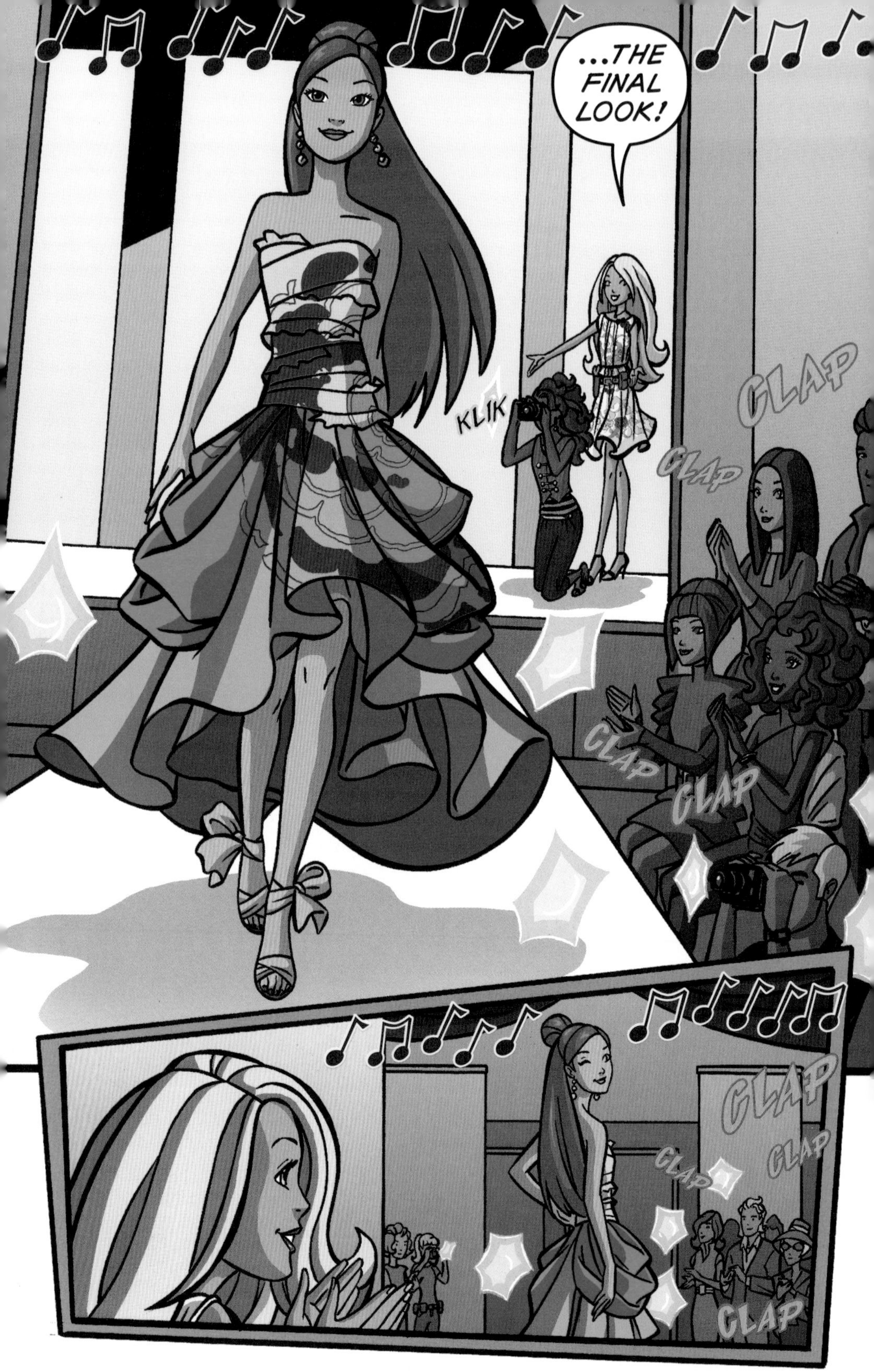
...THE FINAL LOOK!
KLIK
CLAP
CLAP
CLAP
CLAP
CLAP
CLAP
CLAP
CLAP

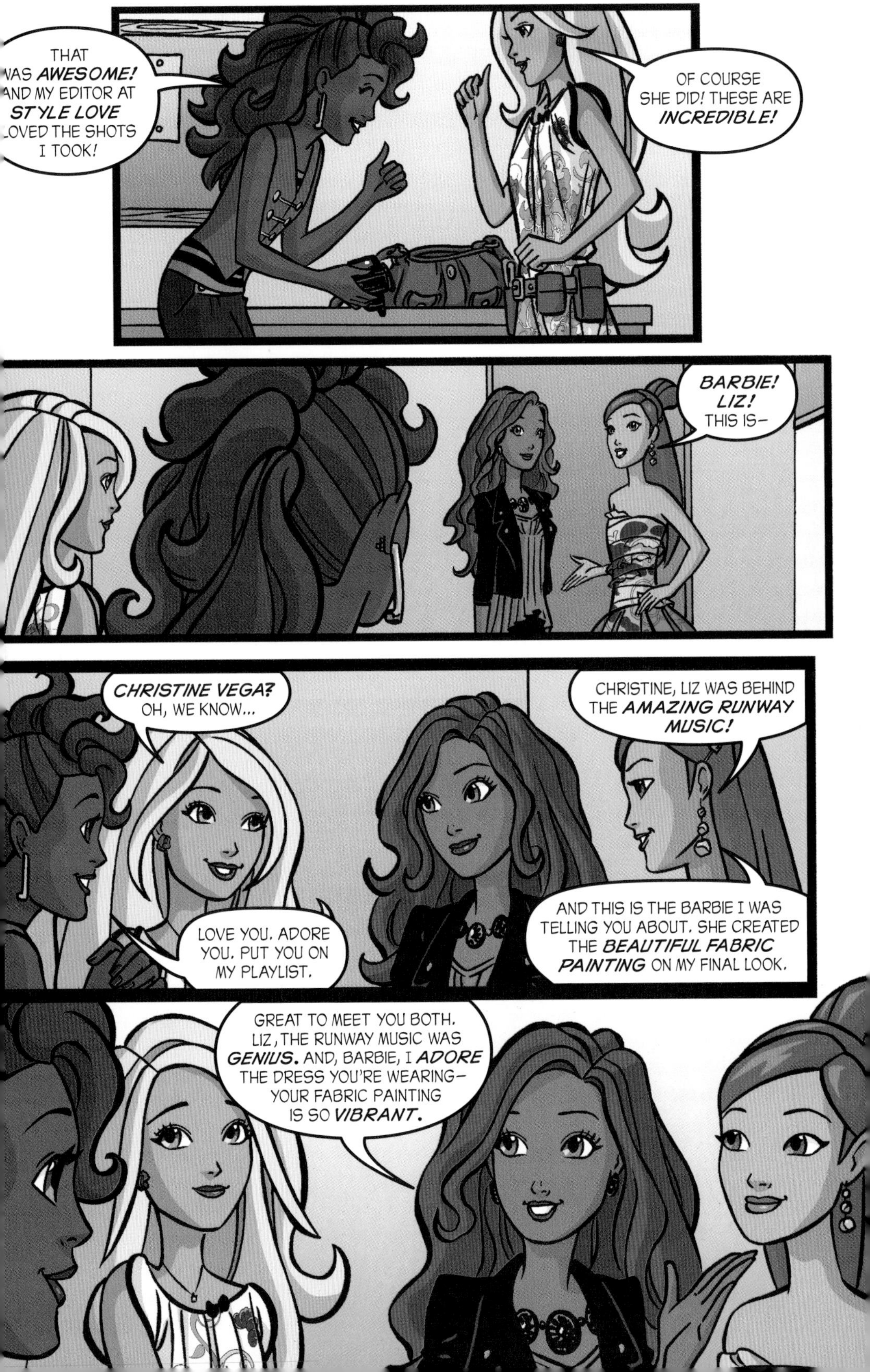

THAT WAS AWESOME! AND MY EDITOR AT STYLE LOVE LOVED THE SHOTS I TOOK!
OF COURSE SHE DID! THESE ARE INCREDIBLE!
BARBIE! LIZ! THIS IS—
CHRISTINE VEGA? OH, WE KNOW...
CHRISTINE, LIZ WAS BEHIND THE AMAZING RUNWAY MUSIC!
LOVE YOU. ADORE YOU. PUT YOU ON MY PLAYLIST.
AND THIS IS THE BARBIE I WAS TELLING YOU ABOUT. SHE CREATED THE BEAUTIFUL FABRIC PAINTING ON MY FINAL LOOK.
GREAT TO MEET YOU BOTH. LIZ, THE RUNWAY MUSIC WAS GENIUS. AND, BARBIE, I ADORE THE DRESS YOU'RE WEARING— YOUR FABRIC PAINTING IS SO VIBRANT.

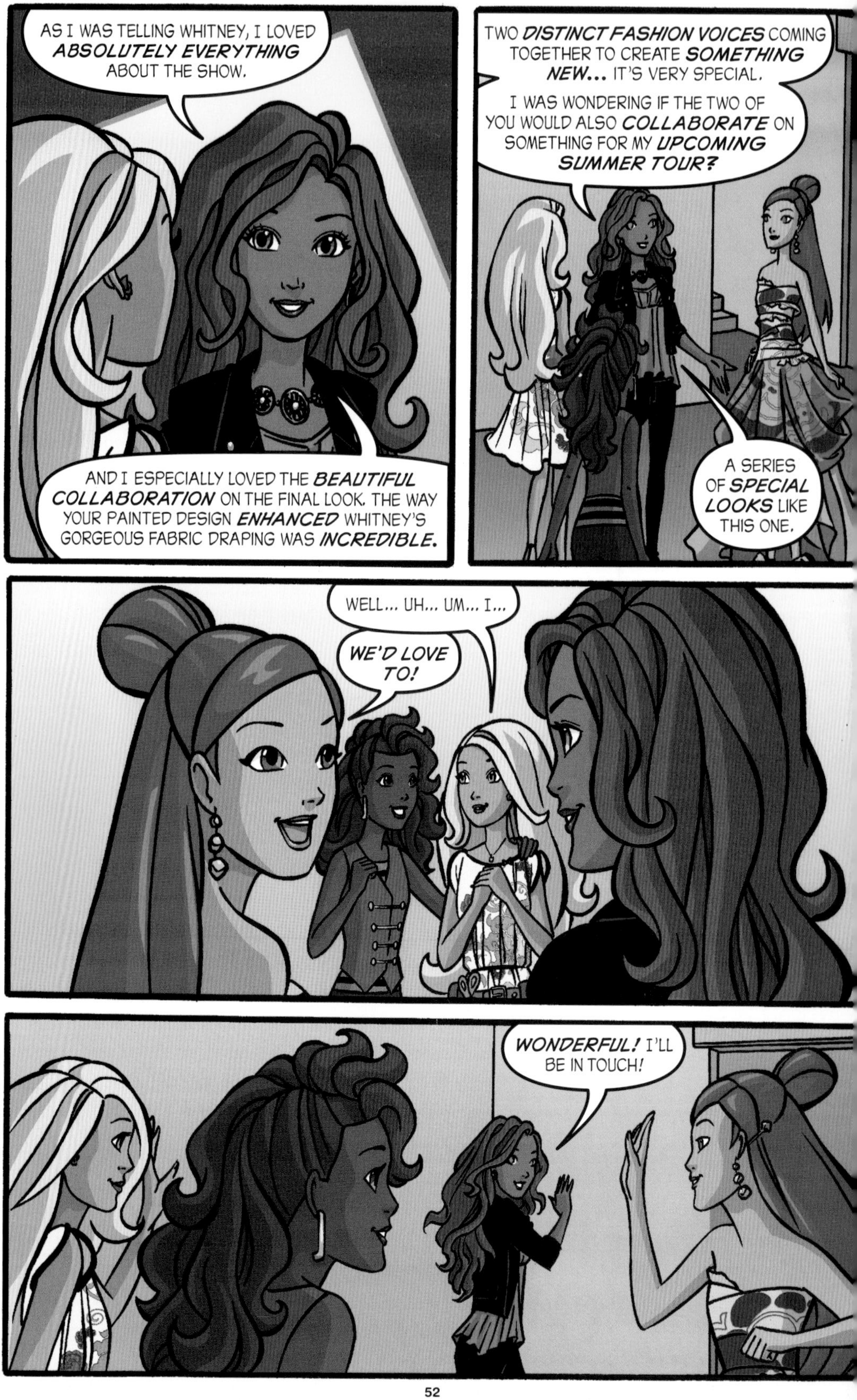
AS I WAS TELLING WHITNEY, I LOVED ABSOLUTELY EVERYTHING ABOUT THE SHOW.
AND I ESPECIALLY LOVED THE BEAUTIFUL COLLABORATION ON THE FINAL LOOK. THE WAY YOUR PAINTED DESIGN ENHANCED WHITNEY'S GORGEOUS FABRIC DRAPING WAS INCREDIBLE.
TWO DISTINCT FASHION VOICES COMING TOGETHER TO CREATE SOMETHING NEW... IT'S VERY SPECIAL.
I WAS WONDERING IF THE TWO OF YOU WOULD ALSO COLLABORATE ON SOMETHING FOR MY UPCOMING SUMMER TOUR?
A SERIES OF SPECIAL LOOKS LIKE THIS ONE.
WELL... UH... UM... I...
WE'D LOVE TO!
WONDERFUL! I'LL BE IN TOUCH!

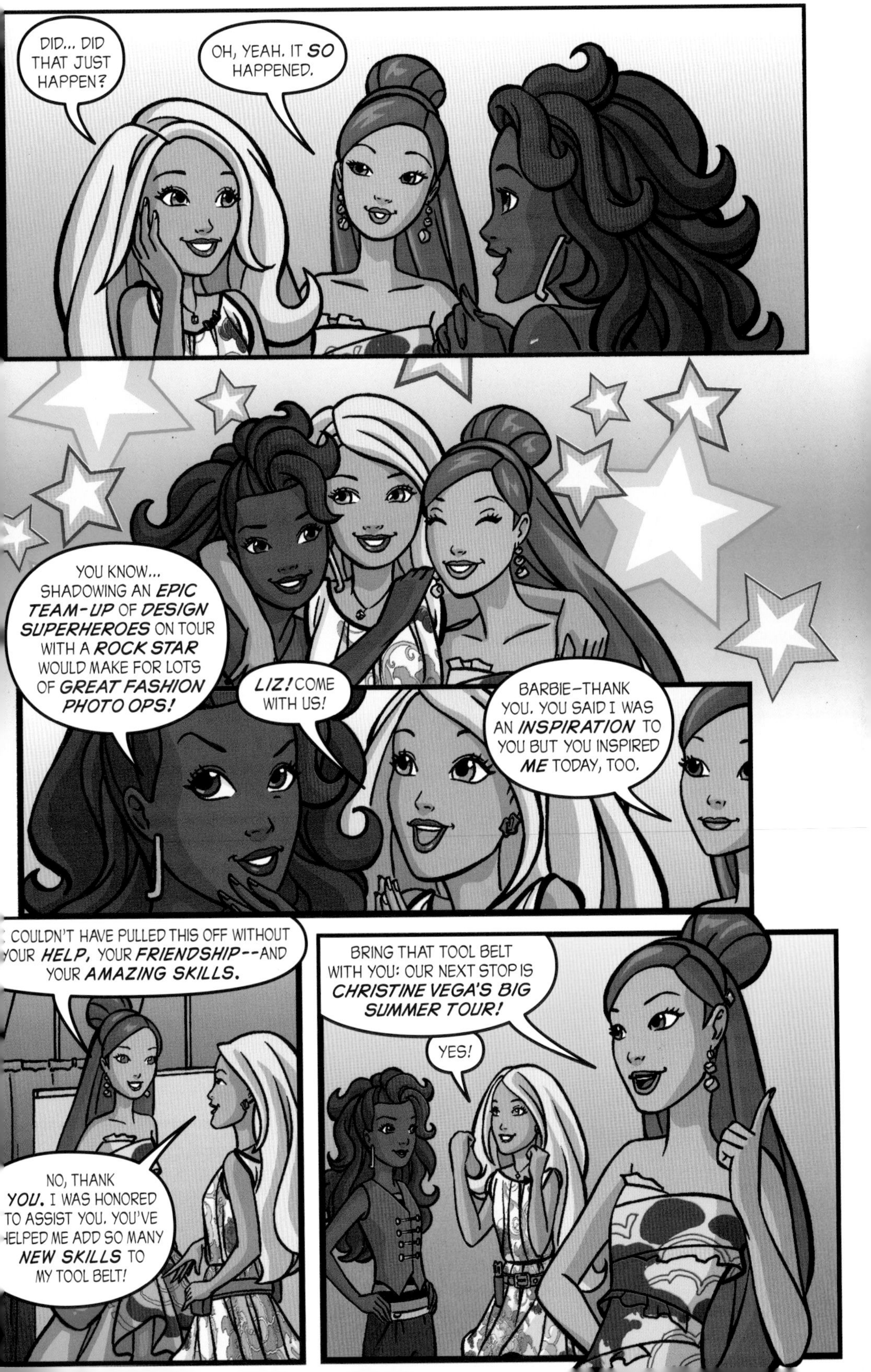
DID... DID THAT JUST HAPPEN?
OH, YEAH. IT SO HAPPENED.
YOU KNOW... SHADOWING AN EPIC TEAM-UP OF DESIGN SUPERHEROES ON TOUR WITH A ROCK STAR WOULD MAKE FOR LOTS OF GREAT FASHION PHOTO OPS!
LIZ! COME WITH US!
BARBIE—THANK YOU. YOU SAID I WAS AN INSPIRATION TO YOU BUT YOU INSPIRED ME TODAY, TOO.
COULDN'T HAVE PULLED THIS OFF WITHOUT YOUR HELP, YOUR FRIENDSHIP--AND YOUR AMAZING SKILLS.
NO, THANK YOU. I WAS HONORED TO ASSIST YOU. YOU'VE HELPED ME ADD SO MANY NEW SKILLS TO MY TOOL BELT!
BRING THAT TOOL BELT WITH YOU: OUR NEXT STOP IS CHRISTINE VEGA'S BIG SUMMER TOUR!
YES!

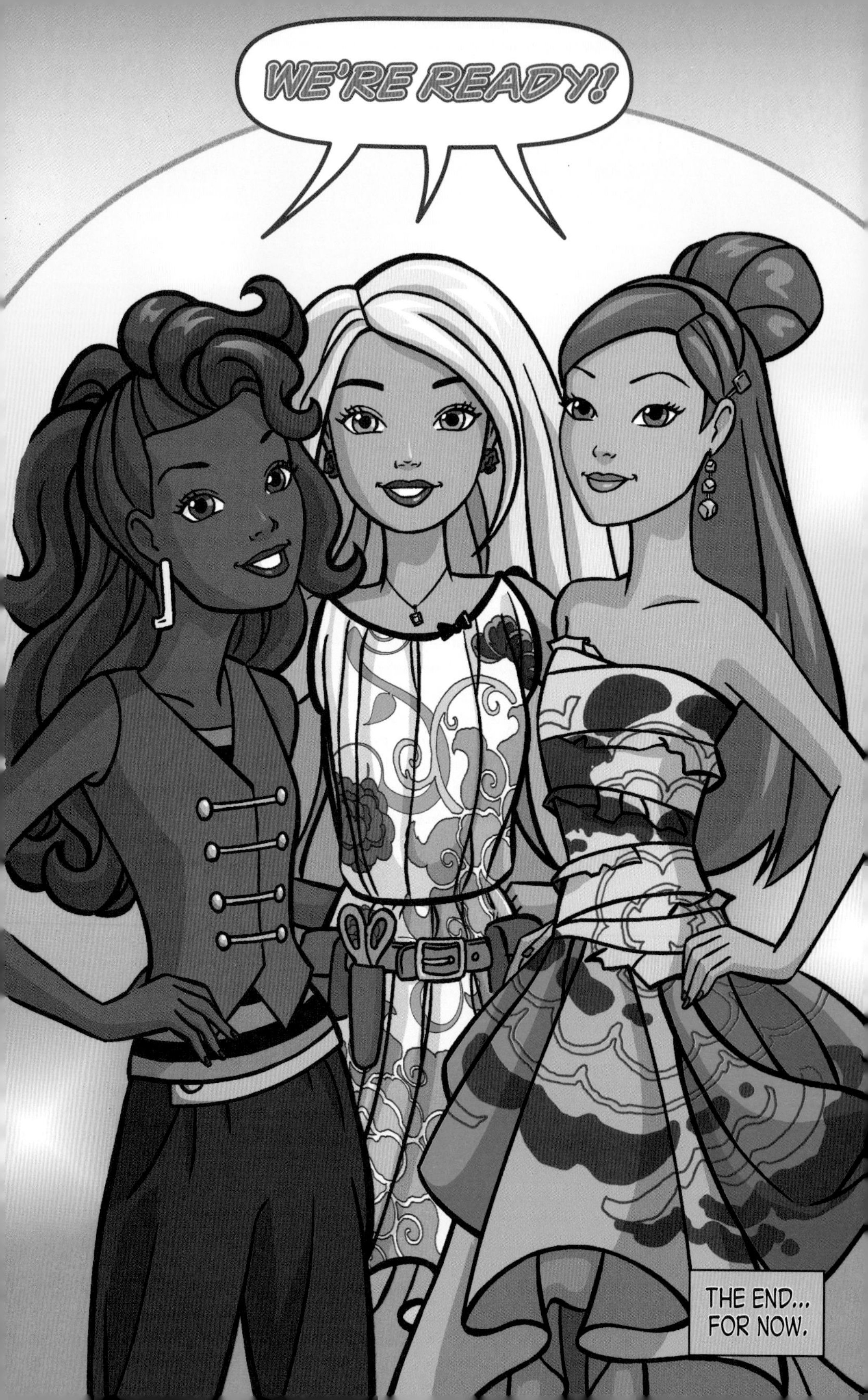
WE'RE READY!
THE END... FOR NOW.

WATCH OUT FOR PAPERCUTZ

Welcome to the first fabulous BARBIE graphic novel, by the comics world's favorite fashionistas Sarah Kuhn, writer and Alitha Martinez, artist. We're delighted you're here to help celebrate Barbie's very first graphic novel.

While this may be Barbie's graphic novel debut, she's certainly appeared in comicbooks before. First there was BARBIE AND KEN comics, published by Dell Comics back in 1962, which ran for just five fantastic issues. Then in January 1991, Marvel Comics launched two titles, BARBIE and BARBIE FASHION. Together they ran for over a hundred fun-filled issues!

While there have been short comics starring Barbie in issues of the ongoing BARBIE magazine, it's been way too long since Barbie's had her own comics series in America. But now that BARBIE is back, there's no stopping her! The adventure started in this graphic novel will continue in BARBIE #2 "Big Dreams, Best Friends." But that's not all!

Coming soon is another all-new Barbie graphic novel- BARBIE PUPPY PARTY #1, starring Barbie, and her sisters, Chelsea, Stacie, and Skipper, along with their pet puppies, Honey, Rookie, Taffy, and DJ!

Speaking of sisters, there's another Papercutz graphic novel that we're sure you'll enjoy, called THE SISTERS—it's all about Wendy and her younger sister Maureen, and how they get along with each other. To give you an idea of what this graphic novel is like, check out the preview of THE SISTERS #2 "Doing It Our Way," that starts on the very next page!

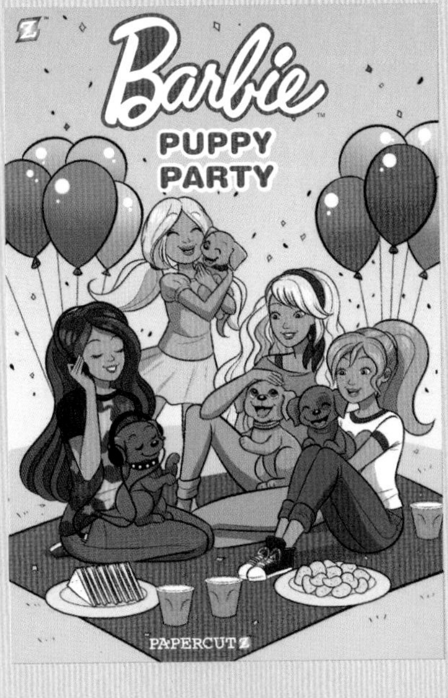
Barbie
PUPPY PARTY
PAPERCUTZ

Enjoy THE SISTERS preview and don't forget to look for BARBIE #2 "Big Dreams, Best Friends" and BARBIE PUPPY PARTY #1 too. Barbie's back in comics, but it won't be any fun without you!

STAY IN TOUCH!

EMAIL: salicrup@papercutz.com
WEB: papercutz.com
TWITTER: @papercutzgn
FACEBOOK: PAPERCUTZGRAPHICNOVELS
FANMAIL: Papercutz, 160 Broadway, Suite 700
East Wing, New York, NY 10038

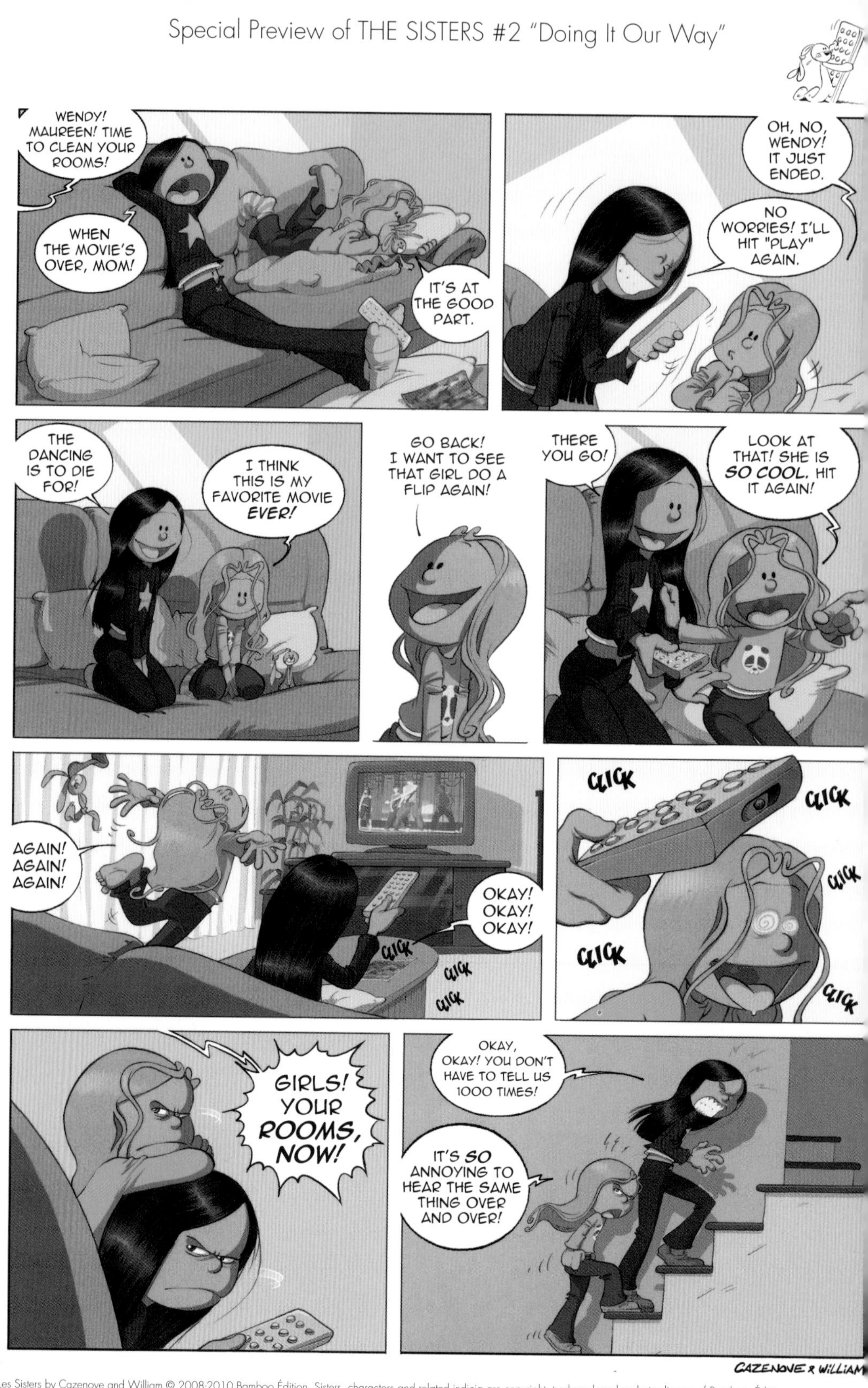
WENDY! MAUREEN! TIME TO CLEAN YOUR ROOMS!
WHEN THE MOVIE'S OVER, MOM!
IT'S AT THE GOOD PART.
OH, NO, WENDY! IT JUST ENDED.
NO WORRIES! I'LL HIT "PLAY" AGAIN.
THE DANCING IS TO DIE FOR!
I THINK THIS IS MY FAVORITE MOVIE EVER!
GO BACK! I WANT TO SEE THAT GIRL DO A FLIP AGAIN!
THERE YOU GO!
LOOK AT THAT! SHE IS SO COOL. HIT IT AGAIN!
AGAIN! AGAIN! AGAIN!
OKAY! OKAY! OKAY!
CLICK
CLICK
CLICK
CLICK
CLICK
CLICK
CLICK
CLICK
CLICK
GIRLS! YOUR ROOMS, NOW!
OKAY, OKAY! YOU DON'T HAVE TO TELL US 1000 TIMES!
IT'S SO ANNOYING TO HEAR THE SAME THING OVER AND OVER!
CAZENOVE & WILLIAM

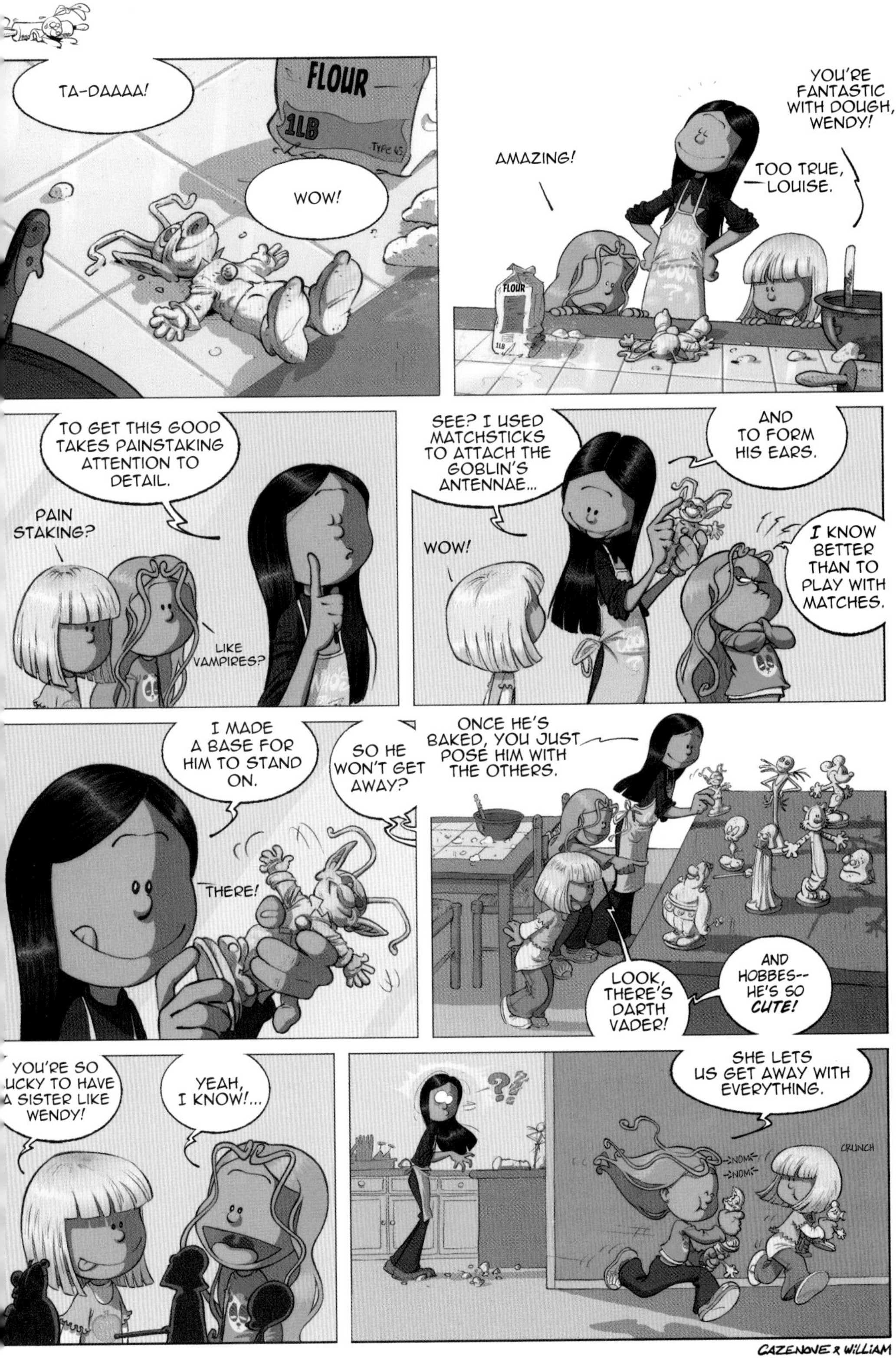

TA-DAAAA!
FLOUR
1LB
WOW!
AMAZING!
YOU'RE FANTASTIC WITH DOUGH, WENDY!
TOO TRUE, LOUISE.
FLOUR
TO GET THIS GOOD TAKES PAINSTAKING ATTENTION TO DETAIL.
PAIN STAKING?
LIKE VAMPIRES?
SEE? I USED MATCHSTICKS TO ATTACH THE GOBLIN'S ANTENNAE...
AND TO FORM HIS EARS.
WOW!
I KNOW BETTER THAN TO PLAY WITH MATCHES.
I MADE A BASE FOR HIM TO STAND ON.
SO HE WON'T GET AWAY?
THERE!
ONCE HE'S BAKED, YOU JUST POSE HIM WITH THE OTHERS.
LOOK, THERE'S DARTH VADER!
AND HOBBES-- HE'S SO *CUTE!*
YOU'RE SO
UCKY TO HAVE
A SISTER LIKE
WENDY!
YEAH, I KNOW!...
SHE LETS US GET AWAY WITH EVERYTHING.
NOM
NOM
CRUNCH

CAZENOVE & WILLIAM

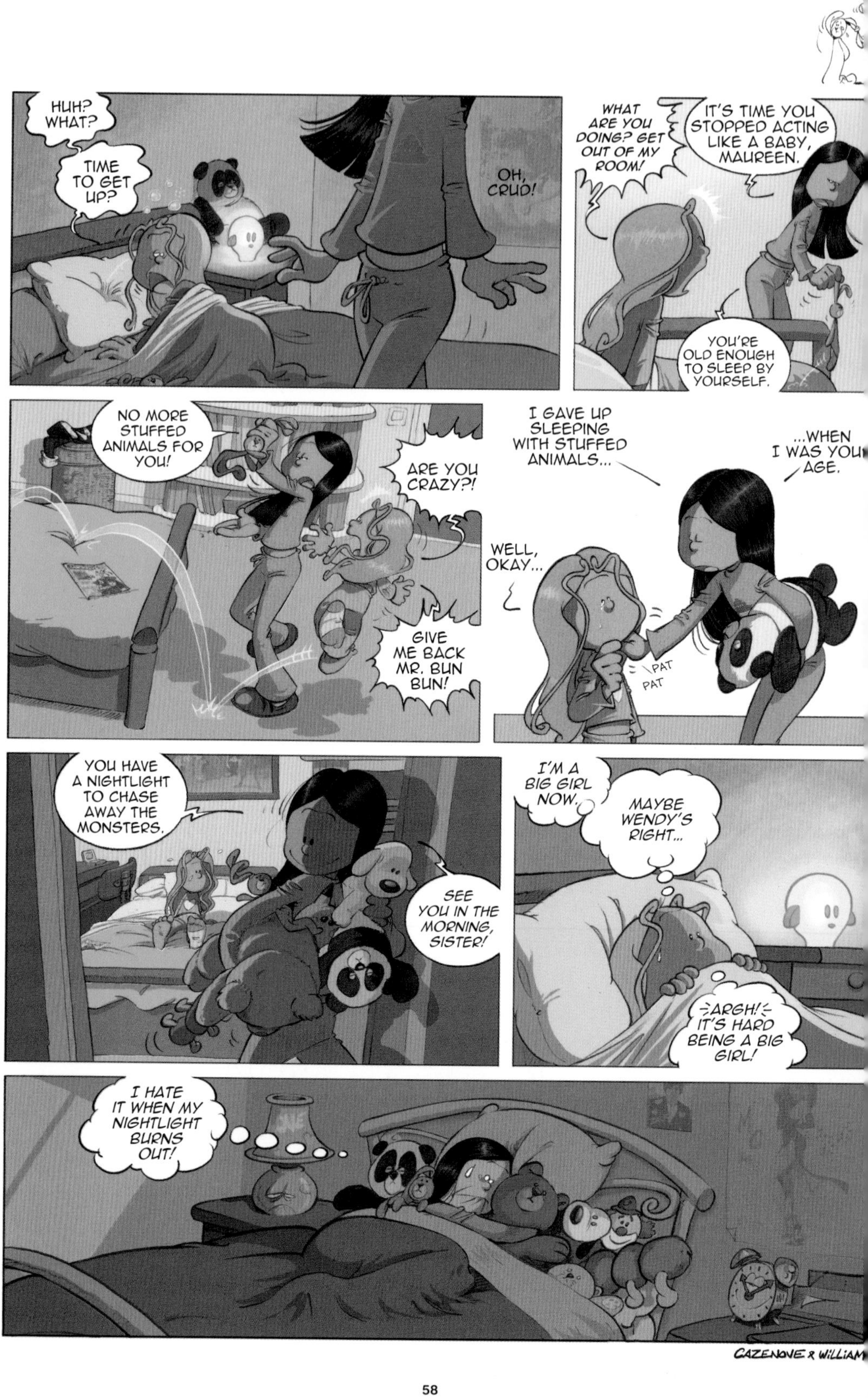
HUH? WHAT?
TIME TO GET UP?
OH, CRUD!
WHAT ARE YOU DOING? GET OUT OF MY ROOM!
IT'S TIME YOU STOPPED ACTING LIKE A BABY, MAUREEN.
YOU'RE OLD ENOUGH TO SLEEP BY YOURSELF.
NO MORE STUFFED ANIMALS FOR YOU!
ARE YOU CRAZY?!
GIVE ME BACK MR. BUN BUN!
I GAVE UP SLEEPING WITH STUFFED ANIMALS...
...WHEN I WAS YOUR AGE.
WELL, OKAY...
PAT
PAT
YOU HAVE A NIGHTLIGHT TO CHASE AWAY THE MONSTERS.
SEE YOU IN THE MORNING, SISTER!
I'M A BIG GIRL NOW.
MAYBE WENDY'S RIGHT...
ARGH! IT'S HARD BEING A BIG GIRL!
I HATE IT WHEN MY NIGHTLIGHT BURNS OUT!
CAZENOVE & WILLIAM

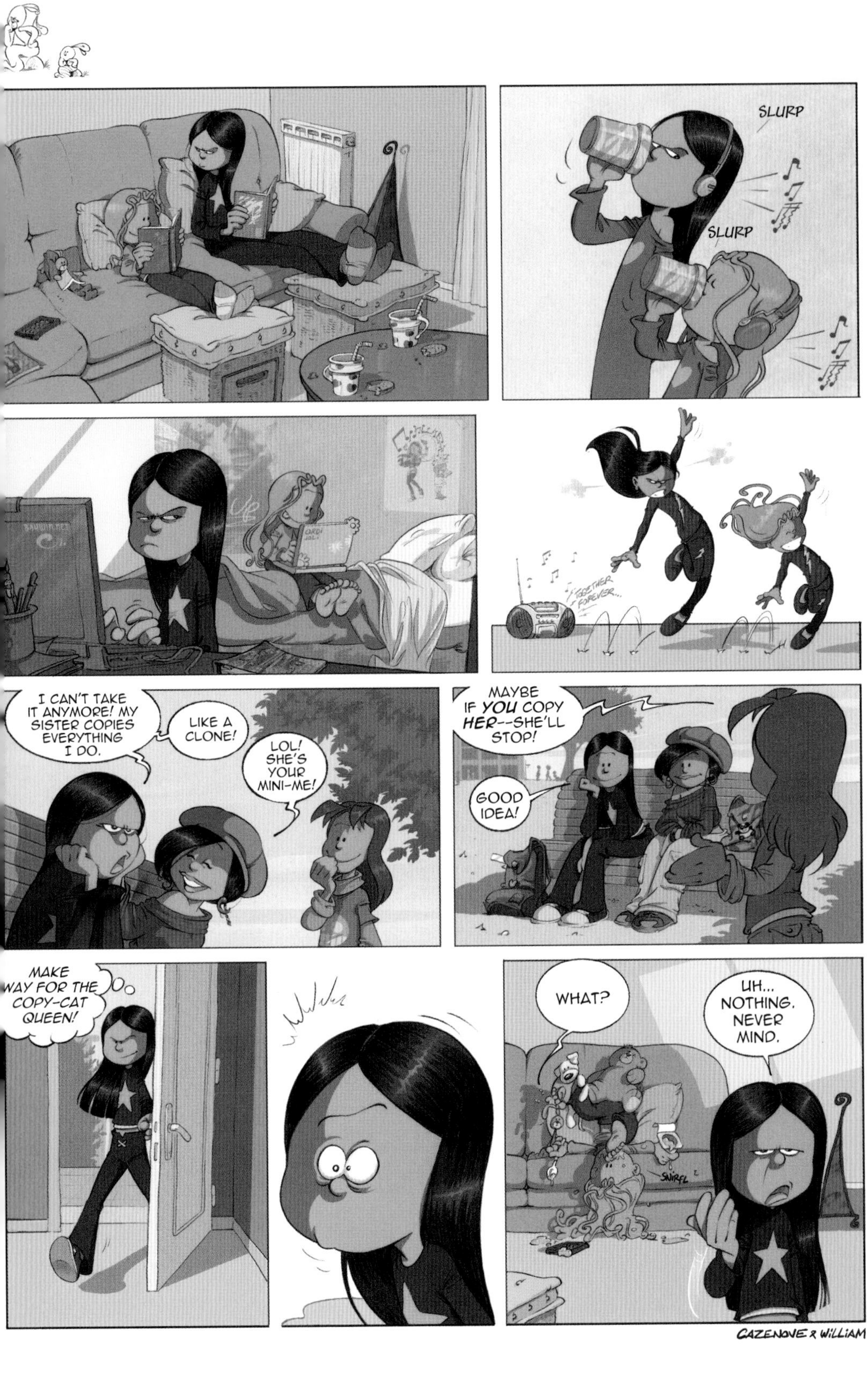
SLURP
SLURP
TOGETHER FOREVER...
I CAN'T TAKE IT ANYMORE! MY SISTER COPIES EVERYTHING I DO.
LIKE A CLONE!
LOL! SHE'S YOUR MINI-ME!
MAYBE IF YOU COPY HER--SHE'LL STOP!
GOOD IDEA!
MAKE WAY FOR THE COPY-CAT QUEEN!
WHAT?
UH... NOTHING. NEVER MIND.
SNIRFL
CAZENOVE & WILLIAM

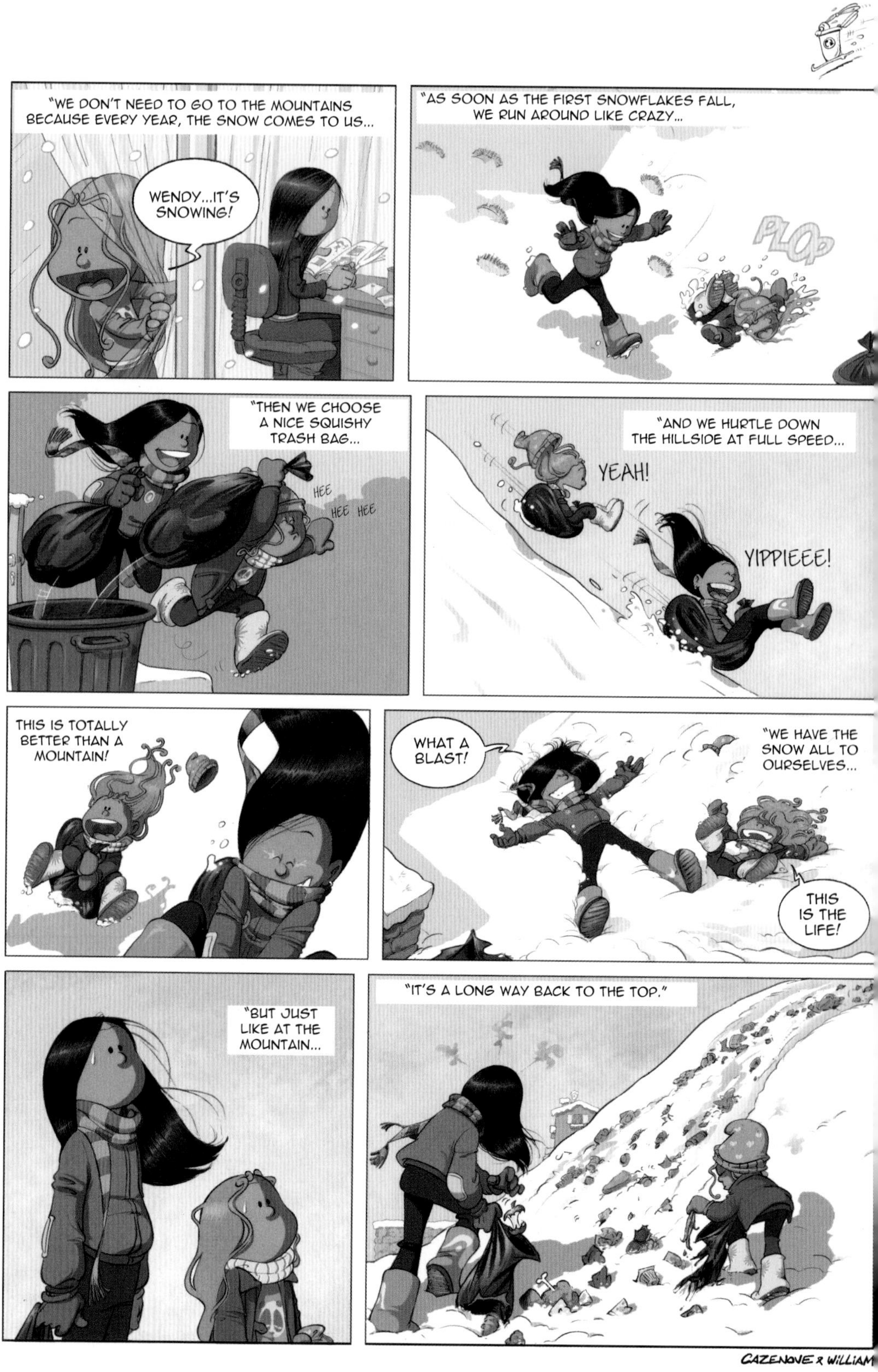
"WE DON'T NEED TO GO TO THE MOUNTAINS BECAUSE EVERY YEAR, THE SNOW COMES TO US...
WENDY...IT'S SNOWING!
"AS SOON AS THE FIRST SNOWFLAKES FALL, WE RUN AROUND LIKE CRAZY...
PLOP
"THEN WE CHOOSE A NICE SQUISHY TRASH BAG...
HEE HEE HEE
"AND WE HURTLE DOWN THE HILLSIDE AT FULL SPEED...
YEAH!
YIPPIEEE!
THIS IS TOTALLY BETTER THAN A MOUNTAIN!
WHAT A BLAST!
"WE HAVE THE SNOW ALL TO OURSELVES...
THIS IS THE LIFE!
"BUT JUST LIKE AT THE MOUNTAIN...
"IT'S A LONG WAY BACK TO THE TOP."
CAZENOVE & WILLIAM

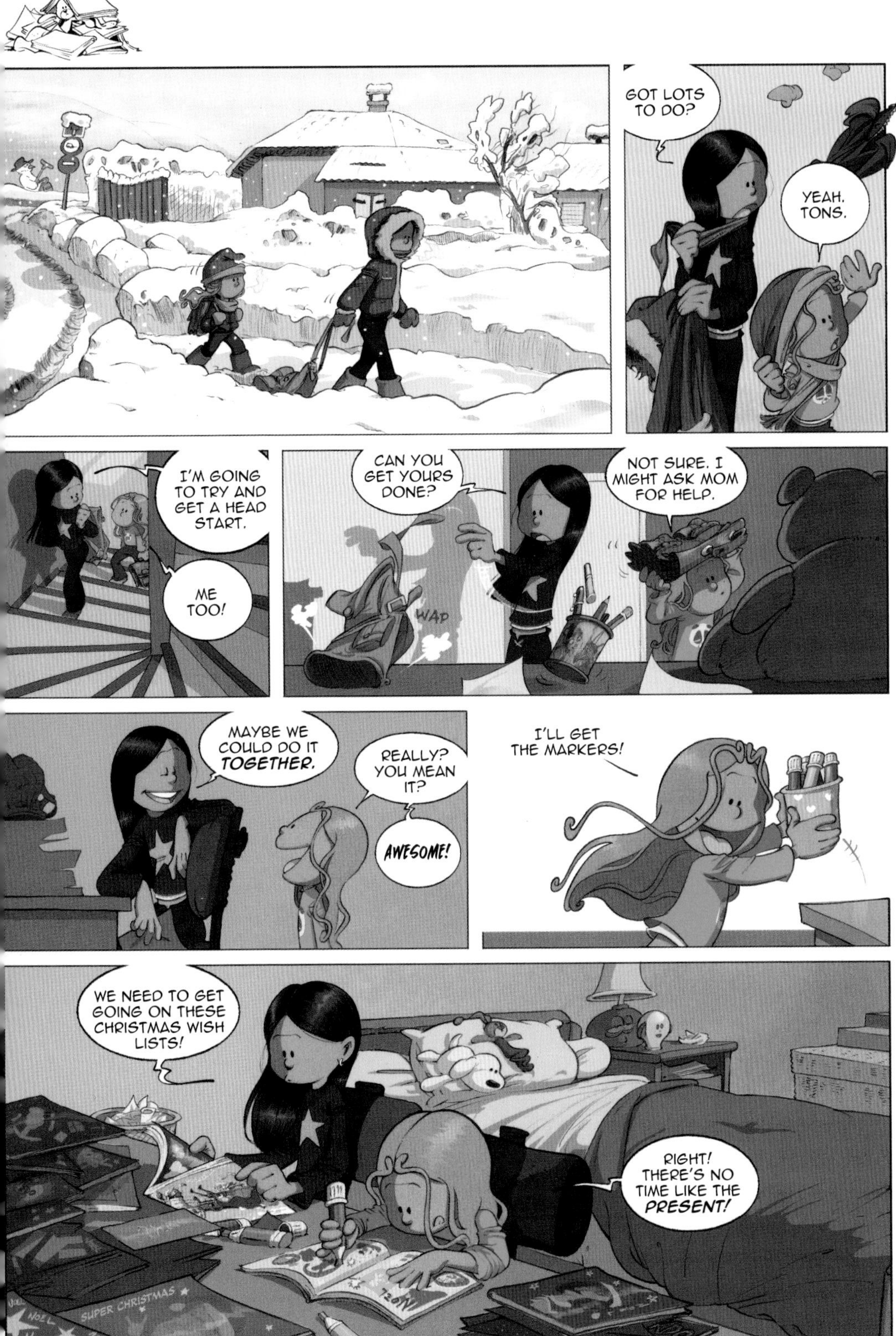
GOT LOTS TO DO?
YEAH. TONS.
I'M GOING TO TRY AND GET A HEAD START.
ME TOO!
CAN YOU GET YOURS DONE?
NOT SURE. I MIGHT ASK MOM FOR HELP.
WAP
MAYBE WE COULD DO IT TOGETHER.
REALLY? YOU MEAN IT?
AWESOME!
I'LL GET THE MARKERS!
WE NEED TO GET GOING ON THESE CHRISTMAS WISH LISTS!
RIGHT! THERE'S NO TIME LIKE THE PRESENT!
SUPER CHRISTMAS
NOËL
CAZENOVE & WILLIAM

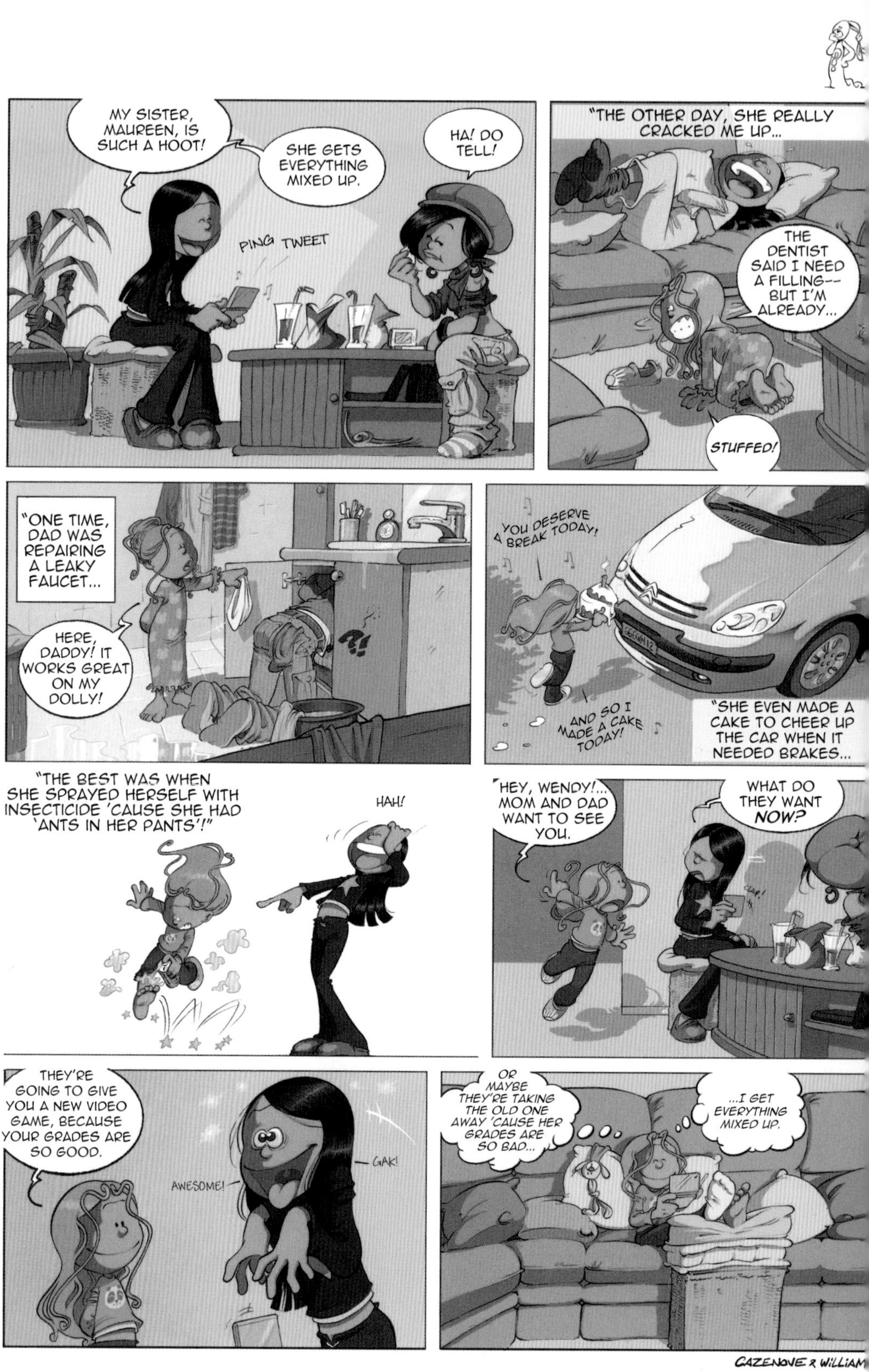
MY SISTER, MAUREEN, IS SUCH A HOOT!
SHE GETS EVERYTHING MIXED UP.
HA! DO TELL!
PING TWEET
"THE OTHER DAY, SHE REALLY CRACKED ME UP...
THE DENTIST SAID I NEED A FILLING-- BUT I'M ALREADY...
STUFFED!
"ONE TIME, DAD WAS REPAIRING A LEAKY FAUCET...
HERE, DADDY! IT WORKS GREAT ON MY DOLLY!
YOU DESERVE A BREAK TODAY!
AND SO I MADE A CAKE TODAY!
"SHE EVEN MADE A CAKE TO CHEER UP THE CAR WHEN IT NEEDED BRAKES...
"THE BEST WAS WHEN SHE SPRAYED HERSELF WITH INSECTICIDE 'CAUSE SHE HAD 'ANTS IN HER PANTS'!"
HAH!
HEY, WENDY!... MOM AND DAD WANT TO SEE YOU.
WHAT DO THEY WANT NOW?
THEY'RE GOING TO GIVE YOU A NEW VIDEO GAME, BECAUSE YOUR GRADES ARE SO GOOD.
AWESOME!
GAK!
OR MAYBE THEY'RE TAKING THE OLD ONE AWAY 'CAUSE HER GRADES ARE SO BAD...
...I GET EVERYTHING MIXED UP.
CAZENOVE & WILLIAM

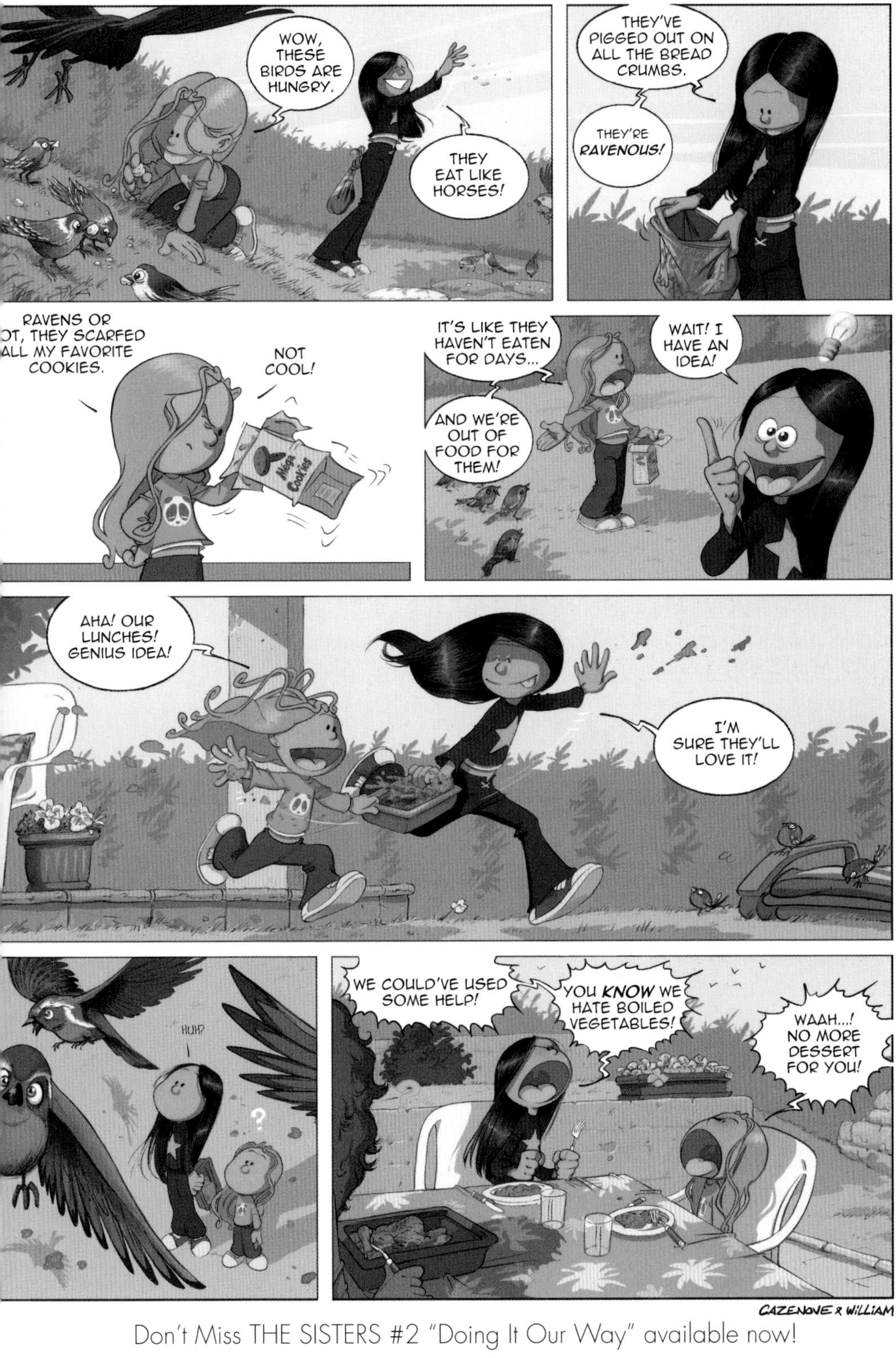
WOW, THESE BIRDS ARE HUNGRY.
THEY EAT LIKE HORSES!
THEY'VE PIGGED OUT ON ALL THE BREAD CRUMBS.
THEY'RE *RAVENOUS!*
RAVENS OR
OT, THEY SCARFED
ALL MY FAVORITE
COOKIES.
NOT COOL!
Mega Cookies
IT'S LIKE THEY HAVEN'T EATEN FOR DAYS...
AND WE'RE OUT OF FOOD FOR THEM!
WAIT! I HAVE AN IDEA!
AHA! OUR LUNCHES! GENIUS IDEA!
I'M SURE THEY'LL LOVE IT!
HUH?
?
WE COULD'VE USED SOME HELP!
YOU **KNOW** WE HATE BOILED VEGETABLES!
WAAH...! NO MORE DESSERT FOR YOU!

CAZENOVE & WILLIAM

Don't Miss THE SISTERS #2 "Doing It Our Way" available now!